WINTER'S VOW

STARLING BAY, BOOK 5

SIENNA CARR

Author's Note

~

Winter's Vow is the fifth book in the *Starling Bay* series, and concludes the story of Dylan and Merry from ***Winter's Kiss.*** While you do not need to have read the first three books, it might enhance your reading experience if you do, because many of the characters in this book appear in the other Starling Bay books.

Note: This book contains a spoiler about Rourke, which can be avoided by reading ***Love Letters*** prior to reading this book.

Starling Bay Series:

Whirlwind Kisses
Winter's Kiss
Maid for Him
Love Letters
Escape to Starling Bay (Books 1-3)
From Faking to Forever
Winter's Vow
Guarded Hearts
Table for Two
A Bouquet of Charm
Christmas Hope

Newsletter sign up: http://www.siennacarr.com/newsletter

CHAPTER 1

*L*ake Ivanhoe was cold in October. This morning the chill in the air near the lake was sharp enough to warrant a thick jacket, gloves and a scarf. Dylan wore his leather bomber jacket more these days because Merry loved him in it. She told him after they had started dating that it was one of the many things that had made her look at him in *that* way.

"Don't let Spart get in the water, Chloe!" Merry shouted, as her daughter ran on ahead with the great big beast galloping in front of her.

"Spart, NO! Spart....NOOOOOOOOOOO!" Chloe's cries echoed across the woods. Dylan got worried. Not about Spart's swimming ability, but because the lake at this time of the year would be so cold.

"Does he even listen to her?" he asked, as he and Merry walked hand in hand towards the lake.

"He listens."

Dylan wasn't so sure, sometimes it seemed to him that the great big mutt ran wild and did as he pleased. He craned his neck and peered in the distance, but, sure enough, Spartacus stood at the lake's edge, not going in any further. "He's listening."

"I told you. He'll never disobey her."

"She loves him," he observed. The way Chloe doted on Spartacus, and the way the huge beast followed her around all day, was endearing.

They strode towards Chloe and the dog. "She needs a playmate," murmured Merry.

"A playmate?"

She winced. She always did that when it was something she wasn't sure about saying. Only, she could say anything to him. Their relationship had developed within the year, and it wasn't until Meredith Nicholls had crashed into his life that he had realized what had been missing from it all those years.

He waited for her to say something, but she was uncharacteristically quiet. It surprised him, that she was being hesitant now, because they never held anything back from one another.

"A playmate, Merry? She has lots of friends at school. I'd say she's settled in really well, wouldn't you?"

"If she had a sibling. I mean, I know the age gap would be too much." She bit her lip.

They had talked about this before. About children, about extending their family. He considered Merry and Chloe as his family, even though he hadn't yet done anything about making it official.

But he had been thinking about it for months. He'd even bought the ring back in the summer, when they had gone out of town. She'd seen it in a shop, when they'd been casually looking at various displays of jewelry. He'd had caught her looking at the selection of rings, and he'd bought it on his next visit, because he had a desire to make their relationship permanent. He wanted to marry her. Didn't see what they were waiting for, except that he was hoping to get past the next few months.

Merry hated Christmas because her husband had died a few

weeks before. Proposing now didn't seem right. Maybe he should have done it back in the summer, but then he worried that it might have been too soon.

Not for him, but for Merry. Though she was strong and confident from the outside, he had come to know that she was soft and had her vulnerable moments. His role was to protect her, and he took it upon himself to always do the right thing by her.

It was better to bide his time, and maybe make a move in the new year. It had been difficult to keep his thoughts to himself because this wasn't the first time Merry had hinted about wanting to have a child. She had mentioned it a couple of times in passing, had planted a seed in his head. He hadn't really thought about these things much before. His love life before Merry had been up and down. He'd had his heart broken, and had concentrated on making his gift store into a success. His non-interest in romance had often annoyed his friends Reed and Rourke, but he hadn't wanted to go down the route of dating, not until he was ready.

And then he'd met Merry; she wasn't only his soulmate, but she had made him see what his life could be like—full, and happy, and joyous, with much more in it than just running his gift store. He hadn't met her, as much as she had collided into him, and while it hadn't been the most fortuitous of introductions, things had worked out wonderfully well.

They were meant to be together.

She was the one.

He saw himself growing old with her. Could see them having not just one child, but two, maybe three if that was what she wanted. Being with Merry, he found himself planning for the future in a way he had never done before.

"The age gap?" he asked, lost in his own thoughts, before catching her looking at him in an odd way.

"Thirteen years," Merry commented. "Maybe more."

He squeezed her hand, not understanding. "You've got plenty of time."

"It's not me I'm worried about. Chloe is thirteen. That's a huge age gap."

He had no siblings, but even he could see that that it would be a huge difference.

She was obviously worried, and it preyed on her mind. He could fix it easily, and he just had to set the wheels in motion. It was only a matter of finding the perfect time; sometime in the new year.

"All in good time, huh?" It was the only thing he could think to say, and he hoped it would be enough.

CHAPTER 2

*H*er new life was so different. Less hectic, more joyous, with a future she was excited about. She wasn't merely surviving, the way she had been in Boston, she was *living.*

This was romantic, walking in the woods around her new home in Forest Heights, holding hands with Dylan as Chloe and Spart ran on ahead.

It was becoming a regular thing now, a long walk for all of them, for a few hours on the weekends, followed by lunch at her place.

How much her life had changed from a year ago. She didn't miss Boyd & Meyer, or the long working days when she would come home late with hardly any time to spend with her daughter.

These days, she worked as a freelance marketing consultant for a smaller department store out of town. Her week was split in a way that worked just fine for her: Monday through to Wednesday at the department store, and then on Thursdays and Fridays she would help Dylan with his store.

He told her that she was his lucky mascot, and that things had turned around for him ever since he had met her. She hadn't done much, aside from convince him to start an online store, so that he could sell his goods online and reach more customers. His store wouldn't have flourished were it not for the products he made. It was the gorgeous, handmade pet feeding bowls, and coffee cups, plates and vases, among other things, that people adored and bought as gifts that made customers come back for further visits, and spread the word by telling others.

She had also taken over the marketing and advertising side of his business so that he could concentrate on making and sourcing his products. As a result, the online store was becoming busier, and she and Laura, Dylan's assistant, shipped the orders and took care of customer inquiries.

This was why his store was now doing better than ever.

The only other change she had convinced him to make was to change the name from the bland Clearwater Gift Store to Fraser's. It was short, and memorable, and friendly sounding.

But this completeness to her life that Dylan brought, the togetherness, the loneliness his presence had erased, had also brought yearning for something else. She wanted to have another child.

A sister or brother for Chloe.

They had talked about it vaguely, and she sometimes threw it into the conversation at times when her desire consumed her. She didn't want to force Dylan into something he might not be ready for, but at the same time, Chloe was growing older, and was now a full-fledged teenager. This had ignited the fuse to the ticking time bomb of her own age. She wasn't too old to have a child, far from it, but as time passed, the age gap between Chloe and a new baby was lengthening. This was the only thing she worried about because things were perfect now. Her life was perfect. This past year had been about a new start for her, and for Chloe, and she liked to think she had made the right decision in leaving Boston and moving to Forest Heights, a place on the outskirts of Starling Bay.

Dylan lived not too far from her, about ten minutes in the opposite direction, and close to the store, but it wasn't ideal, them both living in different places. She longed for something more permanent. Roots, a foundation, a family home.

And yet she hadn't moved just to be closer to Dylan—even though she had fallen for him hard and fast. She had moved because she had fallen in love with this town. The way she felt about it now was so different compared to her initial reaction when she had arrived last Christmas, as part of her mother's carefully orchestrated plan with her friend Hyacinth Fitzsimmons.

Even if things between her and Dylan hadn't worked out, she had a feeling she still would have moved here. It was beautiful, peaceful and friendly.

When she discovered that Chloe loved it too, it made sense to give up her time-sucking career. Leaving the city, and her job there, had been the first step towards a more fulfilling life. The demands of being so high up in a management structure that rewarded hard work and great results had come at a cost. She had missed out on so many of Chloe's school events, but she could see now how she had buried herself in her work after the event that had changed her life forever. She should have been there for her daughter when she lost her husband, Chloe's father, so tragically, and so unexpectedly in a flying accident. But instead, she had kept herself busy at work, and let her parents take care of her daughter.

Now, a year later, she was settled and considered this her new home. Her romance with Dylan had grown and strengthened, and she felt as if she'd met the man who was perfect for her.

All that remained to make her life complete would be to have another child; a baby with Dylan. She glanced quickly at his handsome face. He was looking straight ahead, those now ice-blue eyes staring directly in the distance, keeping watch over Chloe and Spart.

He was tall, broad-shouldered, and good-looking, and when he wore that leather bomber jacket, something happened to her insides; they turned soft and mushy. Her heart would beat faster, just like it did when he put his arms around her and kissed her.

They saw each other every day, and ate dinner together in the evenings at her place, because she insisted on cooking, even when he offered to share the chore. She had missed many of those opportunities when Chloe had been growing up and now she wanted to be the type of mother who made everything, baked cookies, bread and cakes.

Dylan wanted everything to be equal, he wanted to do his share and seemed determined to not take her for granted, but she could see that he was busy with the gift store. He wanted it to be successful, and already he could see that she had helped turn a few things around.

She was content to let him focus on the business, while she focused on being the homemaker, a role she had given up before. But as was often the case these days, thoughts of a child seemed to cling to her.

While she sensed that Dylan had started thinking about the prospect of having a child, she didn't want to nag him about it. Naturally, it meant that they would have to get married first, and she felt like a shrew, herding him into a decision the more she spoke about it.

The only thing that annoyed her was that he seemed in no rush to make a decision to move things along.

She decided to let things lie for now. With Halloween, Thanksgiving and Christmas around the corner, the next few months would be extremely busy.

"What are you thinking about?" Dylan pressed his palm against hers as they walked, following Chloe and Spartacus.

"I was reminiscing about last year, and how I wasn't looking forward to coming here, and how much Chloe hated it once we got here."

"And look at both of you now."

"Things have changed," she agreed. "I've never seen Chloe looking happier."

"And you?" Dylan stopped and turned to face her.

"I'm happy too. I didn't expect to fall in love with this place, and I didn't expect to fall in love with *you*, but stranger things have happened."

He gave her a smile which reached deep inside her belly, spreading warmth to every part of her body. She loved his smile, and his dimple. The way he looked at her and made her feel whole and happy.

She was a lucky woman. A very lucky woman indeed.

But, what if he wanted to wait another year?

They hadn't really talked about getting married, only in vague terms, such as wanting to grow old together. Such as making some plans, about getting a bigger place together, eventually. He had only mentioned the 'M' word a handful of times.

Sometimes she felt needy, forcing the conversation to topics he had never had to think of before.

It's Christmas in a couple of months, she told herself. The season she wanted no part of would soon be upon her. She would wait until it was over with before talking to Dylan about their future.

CHAPTER 3

$\mathcal{D}$ylan stopped by Reed's place on his way back from making a delivery of vases to the home furnishings store. Merry and Laura were also busy delivering his products to the post office to send out to customers who had ordered online. His profits were steadily increasing.

He was happy.

Life was good.

Only one thing remained. He wasn't sure if his decision to hold back from proposing to Merry made sense. Especially since she had once again mentioned wanting another child.

Being cautious, sometimes doubly so, especially when it came to relationships, he sought out his friend Reed for his words of wisdom.

Reed's housekeeper, Cecile, let him in and after he had tasted some of her banana loaf, she let him go to Reed's study. His friend had been expecting him.

It wasn't often that Dylan asked to meet Reed at his house. The Blue Velvet Bar was their usual hangout with Rourke, yet Dylan felt this subject was too serious for him to want to bring up in a bar.

"What's going on with you?" Reed asked, obviously sensing that something was up.

He dove right in. "What made you propose to Olivia?" His question caused the furrows in his friend's brow to deepen. Reed swiped a hand over the back of his neck.

"*That's* what you want to know?"

"I'm curious."

"I hate going back to that time."

He knew Reed didn't like talking about Olivia, but he needed to know. "Sorry. It's just that I'm trying to get my head around something." He wasn't seeking his friend's advice on whether he should propose to Merry or not. He'd already made his mind up about that. It was the timing he wasn't sure about. Was it wise to prolong things because he knew that December was a tough month for Merry? Because, lately, he had sensed a restlessness in her, and he was worried that she might start to think that he had doubts about them. "I want to ask Meredith to marry me."

Reed's smile spread across his lips. "That's awesome news."

"I'm not sure when to do it."

"What part aren't you sure of?" Reed sounded as if he didn't understand.

"She hates Christmas. December is a tough time for her, and with it being around the corner, I had ruled out asking her any time soon."

"So then, wait."

He nodded. "I was going to ask her in the new year."

"It's around the corner," Reed agreed.

"But she seems to be in a rush. I'm sure she thinks I don't have any plans for our future. I don't want her to think I'm not interested in her like that."

"Then tell her what you've told me."

"I also want it to be a complete surprise."

"Yeah. It's not easy, the whole proposal thing, wanting to

surprise them and trying to find the right moment so that they won't guess what you're up to."

"I don't want her to think that I'm not interested. I wish I'd asked her in the summer, when I bought the ring."

"You bought the ring?"

He nodded.

"You knew back then that you wanted to propose to her? Why didn't you?"

"I was worried it might be too soon. Not for me, because I knew she was 'the one' not long after we met."

"It can be like that with some people." Reed grinned and nodded. "What are you doing here? You answered your own question, buddy. You know what you want, and now it's a matter of you going out and getting it."

Dylan pondered his friend's suggestion.

"Just ask her," Reed insisted. "You're only asking her to marry you. You're not actually getting married right now. Besides, it's not December yet. The coast is clear."

He sucked in a breath. It made sense. But given Reed's experience, what if everything turned sour once they got engaged? "What if it changes things, like it did between you and Olivia?"

Reed sighed and looked out of the window. "I temporarily look leave of my senses is what happened."

"But, you must have believed it was the right thing to do at that time? I mean, you didn't propose to her thinking 'maybe' this will work out, did you?"

He could tell by the expression on Reed's face that the topic made him uneasy, but Dylan needed to know, and Reed often had good advice to give. This wasn't the type of question he could take to Rourke in order to get another perspective.

He didn't want things to change between him and Merry. The more he thought about it, the more he understood that he needed

Reed to tell him that everything would be okay, when in reality, there was no guarantee of such a thing.

"Look, if you're asking me whether things change for you and Merry once you propose the way they did with me and Olivia, I can't tell you the answer. I don't know any more than you do. I didn't expect Olivia to change, but maybe it wasn't so much a case of her changing as it was of her showing her true colors. I didn't know her as well as I thought I did. The truth was we hadn't known each other long enough when I proposed. I still blame it on the heat." He gave a wry grin. "It's possible I might have been suffering from heatstroke when I proposed."

Dylan chortled. This thought had crossed his and Rourke's minds back then when they'd heard the news of Reed's unexpected and sudden proposal.

"But you and Merry are different," Reed stated. "Don't let my experience put you off. You've known Merry for how long now?"

"Almost a year."

"See, that already beats the few weeks that I knew Olivia."

Dylan agreed.

"What you have to watch for," Reed continued, "is whether you've had any doubts."

"Doubts?" Dylan didn't recall having any doubts. He shook his head.

"Is there anything about Merry that you don't like, or something that bugs you? Any annoying little thing? Because I guarantee those things never disappear. They magnify."

He wasn't sure he understood the question. "Does it count that she makes me dinner every evening, and never expects anything back?"

"You're onto a good thing," Reed assured him.

"And she takes care of all my marketing."

"You lucky man."

"And my sales keep steadily rising."

"Dude, she's gold. Keep her, hold onto her forever, and never let her go."

Dylan grinned. There wasn't a thing he had ever regretted about Meredith Nicholls coming into his life. Maybe only one thing: that he hadn't met her sooner. He got up, preparing to leave because he'd already made his mind up. He knew what he had to do.

"You're going?" Reed asked.

"I've got something to do."

Reed's eyes widened. "Good luck."

Dylan smiled as he got up. "I'll keep you posted."

CHAPTER 4

Chloe needed an outfit for a Halloween party. Merry had made a note of it in her diary. Her daughter had settled in well at her new school and had a sleepover coming up soon with her best friend.

Merry was working in Dylan's store today. She enjoyed this new way of working. A few days at the department store—a place that was laidback and fun, compared to her previous company—and then a few days at the store.

Things were becoming incredibly busy now. She turned the pages of her diary, and then froze. There was a single word in an entry for December. It said 'Brian'.

Six years had passed since his death, and since then, so many new changes had come her way.

A new life. A new partner. A new place.

There had been a time in her life when the grief had buried her so deep underground, she had never imagined that one day she would break through to the surface and breathe again. But she had.

"You look like you're deep in the numbers."

She looked up to find Dylan at the door. He had changed out of the dirty shirt he'd worn earlier and had now put on a crisp white one, and he had jeans on, which he didn't usually wear while he was in his workshop. He looked so handsome, and she was so blown away by his appearance that she didn't answer straight away.

When he asked her if she wanted to go for a walk so early in their workday, she was taken aback. They usually waited until the late afternoon, after lunch, not mid-morning when they had both started their tasks for the day.

"A walk? Now?" She blinked a few times, savoring his face, thanking her lucky stars that fate had brought them together.

"Spart's lying around looking bored."

"He's a dog, I think he's quite content lying around."

For obvious reasons, they didn't let him out in the store or in Dylan's workshop much, but on the days she worked here, he stayed in Dylan's kitchen area, and they took him for a walk during their lunch break.

"Everything okay?" Dylan stepped inside the room and folded his arms, drawing her attention to them. His arms made her feel safe, secure and loved.

"I'm looking at the figures," she told him, trying to focus on the numbers in front of her, but only seeing the diary and Brian's name on it. She quickly closed it.

"Are they looking good?"

She looked up at him. "Is what looking good?"

"The figures. You said you were looking at them."

"Oh, right. Yes. They look promising. As do you."

"Is everything okay?" he asked, his voice turning softer the way it always did when he spoke to her.

"Yes," she replied, not wanting to share her sadness. "How come you got changed?"

"The vase I was making collapsed spectacularly. It sent clay shooting all over my clothes."

She laughed. "That's not like you."

"I'm having one of those days. Let's go for a walk."

"Now?"

"I need inspiration. I can't seem to get back into it. A walk will help."

She stared at her screen. A walk would help her. She had just pulled down all her advertising data for the past week, and was going to drill down into it, analyzing it properly, but looking through her diary had derailed her focus. A walk would clear her head.

And with Dylan looking so delectably handsome, and obviously feeling restless, she could hardly turn him down.

They grabbed their jackets and set off with Spartacus. The first rush of cold fresh air hit her, and she felt instantly rejuvenated. She let Spartacus off his leash, and he bounded into the woods, disappearing before their eyes.

"You lost inspiration?" she asked as Dylan took her hand in his. "That's not like you. What's going on?"

"Nothing. It happens sometimes. This is better." He inhaled loudly. "Isn't that better? Tell me you don't feel better?"

She laughed and examined him closely. He was behaving oddly. "I do feel better. It's you I'm concerned about."

"I have a larger than usual order for the vases. I guess I feel slightly pressured."

She hooked her arm in his. "Don't. I'll take care of everything else, you just focus on making the vases."

"What would I do without you, huh?" he asked.

She smiled in reply, then told him, "The figures for the online store are looking good."

He turned to her. "How good?"

"It won't surprise me if in a year's time, we're catching up with your regular income."

His eyes grew large. "Really?"

"Really. You might have to take more people on to help with the shipments. Maybe even get someone to help you in the workshop."

He blew out a whistle. "I don't know what to say." They smiled at each other, and he put his arm around her shoulder and reeled her towards him. "You're the best thing to happen to me, Merry."

"That's what I was thinking."

"That *you're* the best thing to happen to *me?*" he asked.

"You know what I mean. If I hadn't moved here, if we hadn't met, I'd still be at Boyd & Mercer working for Dan."

"Does he still keep asking you if you've changed your mind?"

Dan, her previous boss, had been devastated when Merry had announced that she was leaving to make a new start elsewhere. She still heard from him from time to time, and he always said that he would welcome her back in case she changed her mind.

She hadn't.

She wasn't going back.

She was happy here.

Starling Bay, and Forest Heights, were home.

Dylan was home.

He let go of her arm, moved forward and looked around. "I can't see him, can you?"

"You worry about him too much. He'll be fine."

"I see him," said Dylan, then bent down to tie his shoelaces. "He's waiting by the edge of the lake."

She walked ahead, and saw the huge figure of her dog staring at the lake with his tongue lolling out. He was obedient, and she knew he wouldn't run off never to return. "How about we walk along the lake for a good half an hour?" she asked, still with her back to Dylan. When he didn't answer, she turned around. "I said how about we—"

He was standing up now, but standing still, as if frozen to the ground, in an odd pose, as if she'd caught him in the middle of doing something. "What are you doing?"

In answer, he went down on one knee, his hand inside his pocket, his cool blue eyes on hers.

"Dylan?"

He took out a box.

She took a step backwards.

He opened the box while still on one knee.

She opened her mouth.

He turned the box around so that she could see what was in it. A sparkling diamond ring. She gasped, her shoulders sinking with shock. She barely had time to make meaning of it when he said the words she had been dreaming of. "Will you marry me, Meredith?"

She put her hand to her mouth because it was impossible to close. The very thing she had most wanted, he had somehow freakily made happen. One of the beautiful and scary things about being with Dylan was that he was sometimes so intuitive, he seemed to know exactly what was on her mind.

"Meredith?"

She looked at the ring, and then at him, her gaze burning deep. He was asking her if she wanted to share the rest of her life with him. It was exactly what she wanted. "Dylan…" The shock was still strong. She could barely utter another word.

"Meredith, will you marry me so that we can grow old together?"

"Yes. Yes, I'll marry you." A laugh, like a burst of joy, leapt from her mouth, and she rushed forward to embrace him, not caring about the ring as much as what this signified. He almost toppled over, but steadied himself to standing.

"Yes?" he asked, when they were both standing, and had their arms around each other.

"Yes."

He took the ring out of the box and slipped it onto her finger. It fit as if it had been made to her exact measurements.

"Oh, Dylan."

She threw her arms around his neck, and just like night followed day, and sunset followed sunrise, his arms slid around her waist and he pressed against her. Soon, his lips pressed against her mouth and they shared a deep kiss.

The chill disappeared, and in its place, the warmth of being held in his arms soaked through her, heating every inch of her skin.

They pulled apart slowly, and she lifted her hand and gazed at her ring once more. It was simple, one diamond set on a plain band. She loved it. "I love you."

"I love you, always and forever," he replied. "It's engraved inside the ring."

She gasped as she looked up at him, then pulled the ring off, and inspected it closely. Sure enough, there, inside were the words.

I love you, always and forever.

Not only was he a beautiful, patient, and caring man, he was romantic, too. She loved that about him, that he had a hopelessly romantic side to him which wasn't so apparent at first. "It's beautiful, Dylan."

"I knew you would like that."

"I *love* it, but how did you know?"

"I knew."

She tip-toed up and kissed him again, then heard Spartacus barking. They turned and looked at him. He had walked back, no doubt annoyed by their refusal to walk any nearer towards the lake.

"Look, Spart," she said, showing off the ring on her finger. The dog looked at her ring, his tongue hanging out, then looked away.

"He's not impressed," Dylan replied, laughing.

"He would be if I had some food in my hands."

They held hands again and continued walking, only it felt different now. Outwardly, everything was the same, but inside, she felt a deep happiness in her core. A promise had been made, a promise to spend their lives together, a promise of something more solid and permanent, and that made all the difference.

When they returned to the store, she was in no mood to get back into her work; crunching the numbers held no allure. Dylan seemed the same, too, and looked to be in no mood to get behind the potter's wheel.

They were jittery, and excitable, and restless, and trying to act normal in front of Laura wasn't easy.

The shop assistant eyed them both suspiciously. "What's going on?" She stared at one, then the other. Merry slipped her hand inside her jacket, wanting Chloe to be the first person they told. "Nothing."

"Nothing," said Dylan. "I have to get back to the vases."

Merry tried to hide her smile. He had even put on a white shirt to propose. She loved all his thoughtful little touches.

"I'm going to go back home," she announced. "I'll take my laptop and work from there for the rest of the day."

She took Spartacus with her, fed him, and tried to eat her own lunch, only her stomach wouldn't settle from all the excitement of what had just happened. She picked Chloe up from school, then brought her back home.

She'd taken her ring off, fearing that Chloe might see it when she drove back. Dylan was also at home when they returned, and

Chloe disappeared into her room to unpack her bag and put her phone to recharge, doing all the usual home-from-school things.

Merry slipped her ring back on as they waited. "Chloe, honey. How long are you going to be?" Merry looked at Dylan as they both waited to make the announcement. She was itching to break the news; keeping it in had been tough.

"Chloe!"

"She's probably looking through her bag, getting all the homework books out."

"Or she's on her iPad," Merry announced, knowing that the second option was likely to be closer to the truth.

Merry stood up, unable to contain the news any longer.

"Let her be, Merry." Dylan was always the voice of reason.

"I want to tell her."

Chloe stepped into the room and looked from Dylan to Merry, her face somber. "Tell me what? What's going on?" Her voice was suddenly shaky.

Her daughter adored Dylan, and had hinted a few times that she wished Dylan and her mom would get married. "We're getting married!" Merry announced happily.

"What?" Chloe's eyes teared up.

"We're getting married, honey."

"Really?" her daughter squealed.

"I asked your mom if she would marry me, and she said 'yes'!" Dylan said. Chloe's voice bubbled, and her eyes glistened before a few drops fell. Merry was shocked. She rushed towards her, putting her arms around her. "Isn't this what you wanted, honey?"

"I thought you were going to split up," Chloe sniffled. "I really thought…" She reached for her mom's hand, saw the ring, "You weren't wearing that before."

"I hid it from you."

"You really are getting married?" Chloe asked, her eyes brightening.

"Yes, we really are getting married," Merry replied.

"Whatever made you think we were splitting up?" Dylan asked, standing up and walking towards them. Merry also wondered this. They had never argued, let alone raised their voices at one another.

"Don't you know I can't live without your mom?"

The smile on her daughter's face was priceless. "You're getting married," Chloe echoed. They all hugged, and when they pulled apart, Chloe asked, "When?"

Merry shrugged. She didn't know the answer to that.

"Oh, probably not until next year," Dylan replied breezily.

"Next year when?" Chloe wanted to know.

Merry blinked a few times, her eyes on Dylan for an answer. They hadn't discussed dates. It was such a huge surprise, they hadn't talked about anything at all. Now that they were engaged, she didn't care when they got married, because it was the biggest and most wonderful news to know that they were going to, at some point.

"It's up to your mom." Dylan stared at her. "The sooner the better, I think, because I can't wait to marry her."

Had he really said that? Merry was too surprised to answer.

"Mom, when?" Chloe asked. "Dylan says it's up to you."

"We'll see, honey." The things she wanted were coming to be. She wondered what had made him ask so soon? Had it been because of what she'd said when they were out walking recently? Had she talked too much about wanting another child?

She didn't want to push things by talking about dates, unless he was ready to. She also needed time to get used to this, to the idea that she would once again be a wife and a partner. And as for the other things, a family and settling down, having one permanent home to live in instead of her being at Forest Heights and Dylan being at his place, these things took time.

"I should call my parents," Merry said. "This will be a shock to them."

"I should call mine. And I should call the guys," Dylan said, and then decided against it. "I'd rather tell them in person. Maybe I'll casually drop it into the conversation when we next meet."

CHAPTER 5

"*R*eed's going to be late again," Rourke announced when Dylan arrived at the Blue Velvet Bar.

"What is it this time?" Dylan wanted to know, though this was a common enough occurrence.

"A meeting, as always. He's running over, as always." The server came with their drinks just as Dylan sat down. "Thanks." He lifted his beer bottle in the air.

"You're welcome." Rourke lifted his, touched it to Dylan's, before loosening his tie and taking it off.

"Tough day?" Dylan asked.

"It's been a long day. The usual, lots of meetings and paperwork. I hate those kinds of days. How about you?"

"Same as usual. Merry was working at the department store, and I was in the workshop."

"How's that working out?"

"Great." To all intents and purposes, Merry had settled in well at Forest Heights, at her new job, and at the store. And best of all, she had fit into his life. "She likes the slower pace of life. She likes that it's only three days, and working with me at the store changes things up for her."

"She left Boston to be closer to the love of her life," Rourke replied in a jokey voice.

"I wouldn't say it quite like that." While it was true that Merry had moved all the way here, he didn't like to think it was just because of him. She seemed to have wanted a new start.

"How's the online store going?"

Dylan smiled. Sometimes it was hard for him to take it all in. "Doing great. It's taken off better than I ever thought it would. It's all due to Merry." If it had been just him, he would never have gotten around to doing something like that. Merry was the one who had the know-how, the contacts and the confidence to make it happen. "She knew exactly what needed to be done. Someone like me has no idea about these things." He could make the products, set up the brick-and-mortar store, but when it came to taking care of the technical side of the business, the digital space that Merry seemed to be taking things in, he took a step back and let her get on with it.

And it worked.

They worked, as a team in the store and as a couple.

"She seems to have the magic touch," Rourke commented.

"She sure does."

"Seems to be your lucky mascot."

Dylan grinned. She had brought all kinds of good things into his life. "She's the one who said the personalized stuff would take off." He had only done that on an ad-hoc basis, but once he made it a regular thing, putting people's pets' names on their feeding bowls, sales had doubled.

"It blows my mind how much people buy online these days," said Rourke. "Soon we won't have any stores left."

Dylan didn't like the sound of that. "Don't say that. My livelihood depends on my gift store."

"Not judging by what you just told me about the online store."

"But I like being *in* the store. I like meeting customers. I like seeing their reaction when they buy something, you know. Online buying is soul-less. What kind of world is that?"

"Hopefully, automation and the online world won't completely take over the realty market."

Dylan knocked back a few sips of his beer. "I can't see that happening. We'll still need slick salespeople to show us around homes and to earn big fat commissions."

"Hey," Rourke exaggerated taking offense at that. "We *earn* our big fat commissions."

They both looked up as Reed joined them. "Sorry I'm late."

"Business?" Dylan asked.

"As always." Reed slid over and sat next to Rourke, then picked up his bottle of beer. "Cheers." Another toast followed. "I got held up on a conference call."

They exchanged news, shared what had been going on for each of them since the last time they'd met.

Through all of this, Dylan sat quietly, biding his time. He'd sat on his news for a few days now. Merry had urged him to tell his friends on the phone, especially since it was a big deal, and both sets of parents knew. Even Laura knew. But he had wanted to save it and tell Reed and Rourke in person.

But now that he had that perfect opportunity, he seemed to hold back, seemed to want to cherish keeping the news to himself for a little longer.

"Merry's done wonders with Dylan's store," Rourke commented to Reed, giving Dylan an entry point into the conversation.

"Merry did wonders the moment she changed the name of the store," Reed commented dryly.

"What is it now?" Rourke asked.

"I'll tell you what it's not," Reed replied. "It's not the boring old Clearwater Gift Store."

Dylan nodded. "It wasn't the ideal name, I get that now."

Reed pointed his finger at him. "You owe your girlfriend a debt of gratitude."

"Fraser's sounds much, much better," Rourke remarked.

"It's not only the name, she's been handling my marketing, and social media ads for me. I never did understand those."

"And because of that, he says the online store is booming," Rourke announced.

"I am right here," said Dylan, not liking the way his friends talked about him as if he wasn't there.

"Online shopping is where it's all at," Reed said.

"Seems to be, I leave Merry in charge."

"You definitely owe her."

"I know." He cleared his throat, preparing himself. "I know a good thing when I see it, and trust me, I don't intend to let her out of my grasp. So I proposed, and she accepted."

Rourke choked on his beer.

"You did what?" Reed asked, while Rourke continued to cough.

"I proposed, and she accepted."

"You *proposed?*" Reed slapped Rourke on the back in an attempt to ease his cough.

Dylan nodded. "And she said 'yes'."

"Aw, man! You did the right thing. *She* did the right thing." Reed reached across the table and shook Dylan's hand. Then he got up and slapped Rourke across the back again in a bid to still his coughing.

"I'm fine…" Rourke spluttered.

"Get up, you great big, romantic thing," Reed said to Dylan, who obeyed. Reed leaned over and gave him a bear hug. "Congrats. I'm so happy to hear this."

"Thanks."

Rourke was coughing into his tissue, his eyes shiny and bloodshot. "I think the beer went down the wrong pipe," he spluttered, but he managed to stand up and give Dylan a man-hug and a handshake. "Who would have thought that *you* of all people would have been the first?"

"Tell me about it." Dylan was feeling pretty smug with himself. A year ago, if anyone had told him he'd be engaged, he wouldn't have believed them. It never ceased to amaze him how much life could change in a year.

"When did you propose?" Reed asked.

"A few days ago."

"A few days ago?" Rourke exclaimed.

"And you waited until *now* to tell us?" Reed looked surprised.

"I can't believe you're the first one out of us three to get married," Rourke said. He looked sheepishly at Reed.

"What are you looking at me for?" Reed growled. His broken engagement to Olivia was no longer the elephant in the room. He was supposed to have gotten married in the summer, but things hadn't worked out that way. But looking back, everyone knew it had been a blessing in disguise, though nobody actually said that.

"Where and how?" Rourke wanted to know.

"Asked like a true woman," Reed said, dryly.

"It's interesting. I want to know," Rourke protested.

"We went for a walk in the woods, me, Merry and the dog."

"That dog is joined at your hip," Reed commented.

"Might as well be." Dylan had come to regard Spartacus as his pet, too. He'd grown an attachment to the great big mutt, and couldn't now imagine his life without Spart, or Merry, or Chloe. He had much to be grateful for.

"You went for a walk," Rourke prompted.

"And then while we were talking, I stopped. Merry was looking out for the dog, and when she turned around, I had gotten down on one knee."

"You had it all preplanned?" Rourke murmured.

"Of course he had it all preplanned!" Reed shot back.

"Earlier that morning, she was in the office crunching the numbers for the business, and I was making some more pet feeding bowls."

"You're always making more pet feeding bowls," Rourke said.

"They sell, and the personalized ones are selling like hotcakes. He should never stop making them," Reed pointed out.

Dylan continued. "I asked Merry if she wanted to take a break. It was an odd request because we don't usually go for a walk until after lunch…so whether she suspected something, I don't know, but she agreed and we went, and I proposed. She accepted, of course."

"Of course she accepted," said Reed. "Women know a good thing when they see it. Unlike most men. When's the wedding?"

"Not sure. We haven't discussed dates. I was going to hold off until after Christmas, seeing how it's the anniversary of her husband's passing."

His friends both made a low apologetic *Hmmm.*

"I would have held off until January before proposing, but I didn't see the point in waiting." He looked at Reed in silent acknowledgment. "We've been together almost a year, and we both want to make things permanent. Merry wants another child, and it seemed like the right thing to do, the right time to get engaged, at least."

"Do *you* want a child?" Reed wanted to know. Dylan hadn't been one to talk about settling down, and children had never factored in on the list of things he wanted, but meeting Merry had changed all that. It wasn't surprising that his friends found it slightly strange.

It was odd how finding the right person shifted all his previously held beliefs. He *did* want to settle down and make a home. He loved Chloe as if she were his own, wanted to adopt her, wanted them all to be one family. As for a child, ever since

Merry had mentioned it months ago, it had planted that seed in him, he found himself thinking about it more and more.

The idea of a tiny new life entering his world no longer seemed like something to be scared of.

"I think about it sometimes." His friends stared at him as if he'd suddenly grown an extra arm. "What?"

"I never thought you'd be the one who was going to get married *ever*," said Rourke slowly. "You gave me a hard enough time when I tried to set you up with women, or tried to get you to find someone on those dating sites."

Dylan shivered at the idea. "Those things aren't for me."

"It couldn't have happened to a nicer man," said Reed. "You two are both lucky to have each other."

Rourke raised his bottle of beer. "To Dylan and Merry. To good times ahead, and to a baby Dylan," he added, grinning.

"Or a baby Merry," Dylan said. Talking about a yet-to-be-conceived baby made it seem as if these things were almost on the horizon.

"When you set a date, let me know as soon as possible, so I can make sure I keep that time free," Reed said.

"You'll both be the first to know. It's not going to be until next year, probably during Easter or in the summer. We'll have to do it around the school holidays." It had occurred to him that they would go on a honeymoon and would leave Chloe with Merry's parents. Holidays would be the best time to tie the knot.

"We should have a dinner to celebrate," Reed suggested. "We could do it at my place."

"Good idea," said Rourke, rubbing his hands together.

"How about this weekend? We'll make it a Halloween-themed dinner, just for fun."

"Does it have to be?" groaned Dylan.

"I like the idea," said Rourke, looking excited.

They had gotten together a few times recently, him and the

guys, and their girlfriends, Jenna and Leigh. They all got along, and the women were becoming fast friends, which was a blessing in itself. The last thing any of them wanted was for their girlfriends to not get along.

"Are you guys free?" asked Reed, looking at them both.

"Chloe's got a sleepover at her friend's place, so Merry and I are free."

"We're free, too, if I remember correctly," said Rourke.

"Or we could all meet here or eat out?" Dylan suggested, not wanting to put Reed out too much.

"No," Reed and Rourke replied in unison.

"We don't want the women coming here and ruining our Blue Velvet evenings," said Rourke. "Not *ruin,* that's the wrong word, but you know what I mean. It's not as if they don't meet at Books & Buns for their coffee and cake, right?"

They looked at one another. The Blue Velvet nights were sacred. They'd been meeting here for years, discussing and analyzing the things that had gone on in their lives.

As much as he loved Merry, even he had to acknowledge that having anyone other than the three of them be here would change the dynamics of their group, and he hoped that never happened.

"Okay, then. A Halloween celebratory meal at Reed's it is."

CHAPTER 6

$\mathcal{M}$erry held out her hand and stared at her sparkling engagement ring. *Again*. She couldn't help it.

"You do that every ten minutes," Dylan commented. She hastily shoved her hand into her pocket.

"Do I?"

He nodded.

She felt silly. Show-offy. But she couldn't help it. She loved her ring, and she was only just getting used to it. "Is it such a bad thing? I love my ring."

"No."

She hooked her arm through his as they walked around the town square. Chloe was supposed to have come with them, but one of her friends had called her over for a play date, and just like that, in an instant, Chloe's desire to go shopping for a Halloween outfit and to get more Halloween decorations for their home, had vanished.

So, Merry and Dylan had shopped around and bought Chloe's Halloween costume, as well as their own costumes to wear to the dinner at Reed's house tonight. She was going as Morticia and he was going as her husband, Gomez, from *The Addams Family*.

"I hope Chloe likes it," Merry said as they walked.

"Why wouldn't she like it?"

"Because she's a teenager, and it's so difficult to buy for her when she's not with me to try it on."

"It's only a Halloween outfit," Dylan reassured her. "It's not a prom dress." Her heart caught in her throat at the mention of that. A prom dress. In no time at all, prom time would come, too, just like every milestone had so far. Seasons slipped, one into the other, time flowed, life moved on. She had felt emotional in recent days, and she couldn't clearly explain why.

"What is it?" Dylan stopped walking. He turned to face her. Sometimes this man was too in tune with her moods and thoughts. He was able to sense things about her before she could articulate them herself.

Sometimes it was a blessing, and sometimes, like now, it wasn't.

"Nothing. It's nothing."

His brows pushed together. "Was it the prom dress?"

Bullseye. Once again he'd nailed it.

"I'm sorry. I don't know what's come over me. I seem to be feeling all sad, and there's no reason to."

He looked concerned, and she didn't want him to worry. "Was it too soon?"

"Was what too soon?"

"Me proposing."

"No, it's not that. It wasn't too soon." She touched his arm. "I love you. I love that we're engaged, and I want to be with you forever, but I can't explain the way I'm feeling." It was that difficult time of year, filled with nothing but bad memories.

"Young man!" She turned at the sound of the loud, booming voice which came at them from behind.

Dylan groaned. "Hyacinth."

"Well, isn't this a coincidence. Meredith, how lovely to see you!" Hyacinth leaned in and kissed Merry on both cheeks, a welcome gesture she didn't extend to Dylan, and one which Merry felt she'd been on the receiving end of simply because her mother and Hyacinth went back many years.

"How are you, Hyacinth?" Merry asked, out of politeness. It was annoying that Hyacinth had shown up right at this moment.

"When is your mother coming here next?" Hyacinth asked. Merry paused before answering. Her parents had been overjoyed about the news of her engagement and were making plans to come over for Thanksgiving.

"Soon," she said, not wanting to involve her parents in anything. They were only coming for a few days and Merry didn't want Hyacinth to ruin her parents' plans by suggesting they meet up with her. "I'm not sure exactly when." She could see Dylan staring at her from the periphery of her vision.

"Tell your mother to give me a call when she's here next. I would love to catch up with her."

Meredith smiled. "I'm sure mom would like that."

"Who knows, maybe I'll take her to the Fitzsimmons Pizzeria in the new movie theater." Merry suppressed a grin at Hyacinth's obvious boast. "As for you young man," Hyacinth turned on Dylan. "Don't forget. Christmas is almost upon us."

"It's hardly upon us, Hyacinth," Dylan retorted. "We haven't even had Halloween yet. Are you going trick or treating? I don't see your broomstick."

Merry had to bite back her laughter.

"Trick or treating? Me?" Hyacinth stared at Dylan in horror. "Partake in that pagan festival? Absolutely not."

"It's only a bit of fun, Hyacinth. I think you'd look good on a broomstick," he stated, somehow managing to keep a straight face.

"Don't you forget, the Christmas pageant will be upon us soon," replied Hyacinth, ignoring his comments.

Dylan glared at her. "I don't think I can help out this year."

"Nonsense! You say that every year, and every year you end up doing it. Starling Bay needs you."

"I really can't. Not this year."

"Now, now, young man. Let's stop this insane dancing around, and this game of hide and seek that you seem to indulge in every time. Let us rejoice in the spirit of the occasion."

Merry stifled her giggles, though she could see Dylan growing increasingly agitated. As always, Hyacinth was good at steamrolling over his objections.

"We're getting married," said Merry, in a bid to change the topic.

"You're getting married?" Hyacinth's eyes sparked at the news.

"Yes, we are," said Dylan proudly, taking Merry's hand and holding it up, as if he was showing her Exhibit A.

"Well, well. A Christmas wedding?" Hyacinth stared at Dylan in amazement. "That's one way of getting out of doing the pageant. What marvelous news!" She leaned in and hugged Merry, then looked at Dylan as if she was seeing him with new eyes. "Splendid. Congratulations to you both."

Merry looked at Dylan, who stared at her widening eyes.

Had Hyacinth mistakenly assumed that they were getting married this Christmas?

"You both obviously have lots to do. I'll let you get back to it. I expect I'll see your parents at the wedding!" She bustled away before they could say a word.

Merry stared at Dylan as they stood in the middle of the square with people walking past all around them. Dylan was the first to speak.

"Does she think we're getting married this Christmas?"

"She thinks we're inviting her," said Merry in dismay.

"A Christmas wedding," scoffed Dylan. "What do you make of that?"

"That's one way of getting out of doing the pageant." Her heart was starting to tick-tock like crazy at the idea. Hyacinth's misunderstanding had planted a seed. Dylan stared at her. "But that's not ideal, is it?"

"Not ideal?" She held her breath. Whatever his concerns were about not wanting to rush into the wedding, or even talking about a date, Hyacinth's confusion had brought the subject into the open.

"I mean, we have Thanksgiving and then December..." he said.

"But on the other hand, what's wrong with having a Christmas wedding?" She liked the idea of it. She could write over the bad memories for this time of year, erase them and replace them with newer, happier ones.

"You want to get married in December because Hyacinth suggested it?" he asked.

"She didn't suggest it, she got the wrong end of the conversation."

"Do you want a Christmas wedding?" The inflection in his voice indicated his genuine surprise.

"I think it would be lovely."

"Are you sure, Merry?"

"I'm sure." She would rather get married soon, in less than two months, if it came to it, than leave it until sometime next year. Dylan took both of her hands in his. "But you don't like Christmas, Merry. It brings back bad memories for you." His voice was soft, and touched her heart. *That* was why he had held back?

A swirl of emotions swept over her, and she did something she would never dream of doing before; exhibiting a public display of affection. She was so touched by this man's thoughtfulness and kindness, by the way he understood her, that she couldn't stop herself. She pressed into him and kissed him, long and slow.

He looked puzzled when she pulled away, a questioning look on his face. "I should have proposed to you in the summer."

"In the summer?"

"That's when I bought the ring. You won't remember, but we went shopping once, and you happened to look at some rings. I noticed."

She remembered that day well. In her head, she had envisioned that they were shopping for engagement rings. It had been a crazy thought, and one which she had tried to push out of her mind, and now she was shocked that Dylan had not only noticed, but had bought her that ring. "I love you." Nobody understood her like he did, and this in itself was priceless. "I'd marry you right now, if it was possible."

His mouth fell open. "You would?"

She nodded. "You're the one. I can't see myself wanting a life with anyone else. I knew you were the one soon after we moved here, but I was scared to tell you."

"Scared?"

"The handsome gift store owner, unattached and fiercely proud of it. I didn't want to pin you down."

"Pin me down? Merry," he took her hand and pressed it to his chest. "This is me. I'm not like that. I want us to be together forever." His words messed up the beating of her heart, speeding it up, making her pulse race even faster. She looked around, wishing they were in a private place, instead of standing in the middle of the town square having such an intimate conversation. "I wish I had proposed back in the summer. We might even have been married now, I just didn't want to move too fast, didn't want to scare you off. I know you've had to adjust to a lot of big things this year."

"Maybe it's time for me to erase all those bad memories," she said. "Not Brian, I don't mean to erase his memory. He will always have a place in my heart."

"Of course he will," he said, nodding, looking completely unfazed, not feeling the slightest bit threatened.

She didn't want him to feel threatened or to be afraid of her previous concerns about this time of year and what it meant to her. She had experienced many good things in this last year, things which had completely changed her outlook on life, situations which had taken her out of her comfort zone. She had outgrown her initial fears and thoughts about her past, and about Brian's passing and what it meant. She was a changed woman, and she was ready to embark on her next adventure. "I can't live in the past, Dylan. I don't anymore, not these days. I credit it to meeting you and making new memories."

He opened his mouth as if he was going to say something, then stopped.

"Maybe it's time for me to rewrite all my thoughts about Christmas," she said, "and what this time of year means for me. Maybe it's time for me to start living in the future and enjoying the best of what every month brings, instead of living in the past and being haunted by what's happened."

He pressed his lips together as if he wasn't quite sure what he was hearing. "I want you to be sure."

She was sure, facing Dylan with his arms around her, she had never felt surer. "I am. I'm one hundred percent sure. Why don't we have a Christmas wedding?"

CHAPTER 7

"What do you think?" Merry stepped in front of him dressed as Morticia Addams in a long black dress with full-length lace sleeves.

Dylan's breath stuck in his throat as he adjusted the necktie. She looked stunning in that dress, and her brownish-blonde hair cascaded over her shoulders in waves. "You look beyond beautiful."

"I haven't put on the wig yet," she said, brushing her hair back from her face. He stared at her with eyes full of admiration. Heck, this woman had the perfect figure. He couldn't wait to see what she would look like in a white wedding dress.

"You're looking very vampish," he stated with a grin.

"Vampish is different for me, no?"

He nodded.

He'd marry her tomorrow if that was what she wanted, but despite their earlier conversation, now that he'd let things sink in, he wasn't fully convinced that a December wedding was something she would be okay with, not when it came down to it.

"I should drop Chloe off. She's been waiting patiently."

"You do that," Merry said, "I haven't done my face yet. Smoky eye shadow and bright red lipstick ought to do it."

His heart jolted. No doubt she would look even more gorgeous, and once again, he started to think about the wedding. He walked over to the living room to grab his jacket.

He worried that Hyacinth's misunderstanding might have forced the situation, and that Merry's fears about the long age gap between Chloe and subsequent siblings might have cemented the idea in her head. They had both discussed the potential new wedding date all the way home. Was two months long enough to get things ready? They were both busy, and his store had its busiest months coming up. After the initial excitement had worn off, he hadn't been convinced that getting married so soon was viable, but Merry had been adamant that they could do it.

By the time they reached her place, both of them had settled on a date two days before Christmas. A simple church wedding, followed by a small reception would be enough, because neither of them wanted a grand affair.

They had broken the news to Chloe, and her enthusiastic response had filled them with confidence.

"Goodness," said Merry, holding a hand to her heart and fanning it with exaggeration as he slipped the jacket on. "You look delicious. Umm-hmmm." She gave him the once-over, and he had to admit in his chalk-stripe suit and with a pretend cigar, he felt rather debonair.

"Good enough to be by your side?"

She nodded. "Aren't we going to make the perfect couple?" He was Gomez to her Morticia, and—it suddenly hit him—in two months' time, they were going to be Mr. and Mrs. Fraser.

The thought filled him with a burst of happiness, and all he could do was smile at her.

"Are you ready, Chloe?" Merry shouted. Then to him, "If we don't leave now, we're going to be late."

Tonight had worked out beautifully. They were spending the evening at Reed's Halloween-themed dinner party, while Chloe and her friends were having a sleepover at a friend's house.

Chloe rushed into the room, then stopped. "Mom, you look awesome!"

"Thanks, honey. So do you."

They turned and admired the witch's outfit that Chloe was wearing.

"You make the cutest witch I've even seen," said Dylan, and was rewarded with a confused look from Chloe. "I'm supposed to be scary."

"You could never be scary, not to me and your mom."

"Don't forget your hat, sweetie," Merry reminded her.

"Or your broom." He grabbed the upright broom and handed it to her.

"Are you sure you don't want me to come and hang around with you for the first hour?" asked Merry.

"Mom!"

"Dawn's mom and dad are coming with us. Nobody else's parents are."

Beneath that sentence lay the challenge, and the plea: Don't you come along and be the only parent who does.

Dylan chuckled. This daily battle of wills between mother and daughter amused him. It was clear to see that Chloe was becoming more independent and wanting to do things her way, and that Merry was finding it a challenge to remember that her daughter wasn't so young and dependent on her anymore. Chloe wasn't an insolent, bad-tempered teen, but she was headstrong, and she often challenged Merry.

He stepped in. "She'll be fine, Merry. Dawn's parents have taken on the responsibility and there are ten girls." He winked at Chloe, who smiled back.

Merry ran a hand over her forehead. "Is it safe here?"

"Is it safe here?" he repeated. "How long have you lived here now? Everyone knows mostly everyone. She'll be fine."

"Yeah, Mom, listen to Dylan. He knows. I'll be okay."

"Are you sure you don't want to come along with me to see Chloe off?" Dylan asked, not wanting Merry to worry.

"I have to put on the wig and do my makeup."

"Okay."

"'Bye, Mom," Chloe kissed her mom.

"Call me if you need anything, or if you want to come home."

"I won't, Mom. These are my friends. It's going to be fun."

Dylan understood. It was Chloe's first sleepover in Starling Bay. Settling in here had been fine, because the only thing Merry had been concerned about had been Chloe and how she would fit in and make friends.

Sometimes, he wondered if Merry worried too much.

Chloe told him, sometimes when the two of them talked, that her mom was different now, gentler, and had more time for her. He had come to realize just how much the child had missed her mother. He had never mentioned this to Merry, because he didn't want to hurt her, but in a way he sensed that she already knew.

He had been driving for a good few minutes, listening to the loud music on the radio; Chloe had turned the volume up high. He turned it down enough so that they could talk.

"Are you nervous about trick or treating?" he asked.

"No, why would I be nervous?"

"Oh, you know, being in a new area with new friends. This being your first time trick or treating over here, not that you can't handle it," he said quickly. "I know you can handle anything, but, you know, it's okay to admit to feeling a little nervous."

"I'm not nervous."

"You know the girls pretty well, huh?"

"Yeah. Dawn's really nice. She says I'm her best friend. I

don't believe her, 'cause she hasn't known me that long, but she's nice."

Smart cookie, he thought.

"How do you feel about me and your mom getting married, and having the wedding so soon?" This was what he was most curious to learn.

She was silent, which prompted him to glance at her, but she was texting, thank goodness.

"Chloe! What did we say about the phone? No texting when you're in a conversation with other people."

"Dawn texted to ask me how long I would be."

"Tell her we'll be there in another five to six minutes."

"So, as I was asking, how do you feel about me and your mom getting married so close to Christmas?"

She wrinkled her nose. "It's not so soon. You've been dating for years."

Years? He chuckled. "It's coming up to one year."

"That's *long*."

"Do you need more time to get used to the idea?"

"Of you being my new dad?"

He frowned, not knowing what to say to that. He needed to say something. "I'll never take the place of your dad, Chloe. I can't be him, but I'll do my best to be there for you."

She looked down at her hands. The phone was nowhere in sight.

"Chloe?"

"Hmmm."

What was he doing? He wanted to gauge her reaction, her mood and her attitude to their impending wedding. Of course Merry had also asked her, but Dylan sensed that Chloe sometimes told her mom what she thought Merry wanted to hear. She seemed to be more candid and open with him.

"You make mom laugh. She never used to laugh much before, and now she laughs almost every day."

He glanced at her. If ever there was a confirmation that she was okay with it, it didn't come any clearer than this. "She laughs every day, huh?"

Chloe nodded. "She laughs a lot. She laughs so much I can see wrinkles at the corners of her eyes."

That made him laugh.

"Don't tell her I said that," pleaded Chloe.

"I won't. I don't think she'd mind, even if she heard you."

"You love her lots, don't you?"

"I love her more than you can imagine."

Chloe smiled, a huge, all-encompassing smile. It pained his heart, and lifted him at the same time, this bittersweet moment which told him that this child was so overjoyed to see her mom happy again. "I want us to be one happy family. I want you to stay with us and not go home every day. I want us to have a nice Christmas, and we will, if you get married two days before."

"I'd marry your mom in an instant, Chloe."

She giggled, and it made him giggle.

CHAPTER 8

*W*ho would have thought that dressing up for Halloween was so much fun? Especially for adults. Granted, it was only a dinner and not a party, but still, having to dress up for the occasion made it so much more exciting.

By the time Dylan came back from dropping Chloe off, Merry had put on her Morticia wig and makeup.

He walked in, then stopped and took in her appearance, and a delicious smile spread across his lips. "You look hot."

She raised her eyebrow provocatively, placed a hand on her hip, and leaned against the wall in her sexiest pose. "Hot, did you say?" she purred, in her best and most seductive voice. Then she burst out laughing because she felt so ridiculous. "I can't do sexy."

He walked towards her. "You don't need to do sexy, because you already are, and you don't even know it. Wearing that dress…" He made an approving noise in the back of his throat as he slipped his arm around her waist and lowered his head down to kiss her.

"My lipstick!" she shrieked, backing off.

"That's never stopped you before."

"Later," she said, touching his lips gently with her finger. "But now, we should go. Jenna said for us to not be late. We have a lot of catching up to do. She's excited."

"About the dinner?"

"About our engagement. She and Leigh both are." Merry had become good friends with the two women, and this had helped make her settling into Starling Bay all the more easier. It hadn't been easy to leave behind her friends, her work, and the home where there had been so many memories of her life. Moving away to a new town and a new beginning wasn't something she would ever have dreamt of doing before, yet somehow, after meeting Dylan, it seemed to be the natural progression for her.

"Are we going to tell everyone about the wedding?" Her friends had been ecstatic when she had told them about Dylan's proposal. This latest development would be even bigger.

"I don't see that we have a choice. If this is what we've decided—"

"We have." How was it that she was so sure of this, and Dylan was the one who seemed to hesitate?

"Then we should tell them, after all, we don't have long. Are you really sure, Merry?"

They still had to check out possible venues, they had to make firm plans, they had to do all the paperwork, but, barring any of those things causing problems, there was no reason they couldn't get married before Christmas.

"How do I convince you that I'm sure?" she asked him.

"I thought you women liked to plan for months and months? Will we have enough time?"

"We've already said that we want to keep it small and simple." She'd been married before, but this was his first wedding. She was worried that he was agreeing to things she wanted. "It depends on what you want."

He gazed into her eyes. "I want whatever you want."

"But it's your first wedding."

"And it will be my only wedding," he replied.

She bit her lip. It was all well and good to say things like that, but as life had shown her, things didn't always go according to plan. He must have realized what he had said, for he kissed the back of her hand and then her lips, and said, "Sorry. I didn't mean that."

"You never know what's around the corner," she murmured. "That's why I say, don't put off until tomorrow what you can do today."

"I can't marry you today, Merry," he said, laughing, taking away some of the somberness that had crept into the mood. "I would if I could, but we need guests, the people we love to be here. And you need a dress, and I need a fancy suit."

"I know. I get it. I'm kidding. But it's true. I don't want to waste time." Having experienced the death of her husband, and seeing the devastation it had caused as their tiny family was left bereft, had taught her a few life lessons. It was why she hadn't waited long to leave Boston and move here.

It was why wanting to set down roots again now was so important.

"What do you want?" he asked.

"A simple blessing and some food, and then it's done." She didn't want a fancy venue, or tables full of flowers, just one bouquet for her to hold. A simple wedding dress. No band or musicians, no fancy four-tiered cake. Just a simple one that she might ask Leigh to make. "There isn't much to organize, especially since we're keeping it small."

"So, are we settling on that date?" he asked.

"I want to. And I'll be fine," she said, squeezing his arms, as he pressed his forehead against hers.

"Married in less than two months," he commented.

"Yes," she whispered.

He stood up straight, breathed out, and smoothed down his jacket before holding his arm out for her. "Shall we?"

"Let's." She glanced back over her shoulder and made an apologetic face at Spartacus who had a sorry look on his face. "Sorry, Spart," she said, as they closed the door behind them.

"You said we had to dress up!" Rourke protested as they all walked in.

She and Dylan had arrived at Reed's mansion as the same time as Rourke and Leigh did, and all six of them congregated in the great hallway. They had all dressed up except for Reed.

"That's not fair," Dylan protested.

"I'm the host," said Reed. He was wearing black pants and a black shirt. "I'm wearing all black. That's ghoulish enough."

"You might be all in black, but still, that's lame," Rourke said. He had made a real effort, and had shown up in a scary joker costume complete with the garish makeup. It was a good thing Merry didn't have a fear of clowns, otherwise she would have found it difficult to sit through dinner.

"Do you have any idea how long it took me to paint my face?" he moaned. "I don't know how you women do it every day."

At this, the women laughed.

"We don't paint our faces that much," Jenna shot back. "But I applaud the effort."

"At least Jenna made an effort," Rourke said.

"Thank you," said Jenna, taking a bow. She had. She was in a long, slinky black dress and a witch's hat, and had greeted them all at the door with her broom in her hand.

"A graveyard bride," commented Dylan. Leigh wore a gothic

wedding dress, with a black rose veil, and her face done up somewhat pale with smoky black eye shadow.

"You look amazing," Merry told her.

"Thank you, so do you."

"Shall we move out of the hallway?" Reed suggested and led them into his living room, where his butler, Pennington, walked around with a tray of champagne flutes. The table was set out with lots of little canapes, courtesy of Cecile, Reed's cook, no doubt.

Merry was relieved to see that the food wasn't Halloween themed. No gory-looking appetizers, thank goodness.

"But first, a toast and congratulations to the happy couple," said Reed, lifting his glass. "To Dylan and Merry on their engagement."

They all raised their glasses, and congratulated her and Dylan. It was an odd sight, this coterie of friends dressed up like this, congratulating them. A moment so surreal, it might as well have been a dream.

Soon enough, the guys congregated together, while Merry, along with Jenna and Leigh, formed a group of their own. Her friends had a million questions about how Dylan had proposed, and then they asked her if she had thought about the wedding or the dress. Jenna told her that there was only one place she could go to get the perfect wedding dress.

Her friends seemed surprised when Merry told them she wanted a small affair and nothing ostentatious. "I've had all of that before. The big wedding, the expensive dress…"

Her friends fell silent.

"I had all of that with Brian," Merry continued. "I don't want to have something so grand this time around."

"I don't blame you. I wouldn't want a big expensive wedding either. You're entitled to have the type of wedding *you* want. It's your big day," Jenna said.

"Let me know if I can help in any way," offered Leigh.

"I did mean to ask you." Merry hesitated before asking and wondered if it would it be impertinent to make this request of her new friend.

"Sure, ask away. I'd love to help."

"I was hoping you might bake the wedding cake for us."

Leigh clapped her hands together. "I would *love* to make your wedding cake. Are you sure you want me to do it? I'm not a specialist wedding cake baker."

"Of course I'm sure. I love the handmade cakes at the bookshop. I would love you to make our wedding cake, and it doesn't have to be a fruitcake. Chloe loves chocolate, and so do I."

Leigh beamed with happiness. "Nearer to the time, we'll get together and discuss ideas."

"What about dress ideas?" Jenna asked. "We'll have to go shopping for the dress together when you've decided on the date."

"I haven't had much chance to think about it." She and Dylan were only just getting used to the idea of a Christmas wedding. She hadn't thought about the dress. "I want something simple," she said, now that she had been forced to consider it. "But something elegant, and fitted, no meringue-shaped dress, nothing big, nothing fancy, no tulle effect."

Jenna and Leigh exchanged glances. "Understated glamor, I think, is what we call it." Leigh nodded her head at Merry. "That's definitely you."

"Whenever you're ready. We have plenty of time," said Jenna. "Reed said you were looking to get married next year."

"That's what we had decided," said Merry. She glanced over at Dylan, hoping to catch his eye, but he appeared to be deep in conversation with the guys. Before she was able to hint at the change of date, Jenna started talking about her friend Shay, with whom she had lived when she had first come to Starling Bay.

Merry listened to the conversation, lost in her own thoughts. With Jenna and Leigh talking about specifics, the dress and the cake, things were becoming very real, and she didn't have long to get everything organized.

After a while, their hosts announced that it was time for dinner, and they all went into the formal dining room. She naturally gravitated towards Dylan, until she saw the place settings on the long oval-shaped table.

A collective 'What?' went around the room as everyone realized at the same time. Reed and Jenna had smiles on their faces.

"That's right," said Reed. "We're going to mix it up a little. You ladies can't sit together, and neither can us guys, and you're not allowed to sit with your partners either."

She and Dylan glanced at one another. It was a great idea. She appreciated that Reed and Jenna had gone to such trouble. Not only the dressing up in a Halloween-themed outfit, but the way the mansion was decorated with Halloween decorations in the hallway and outside.

She sat across from Dylan, in between Reed and Rourke with Leigh next to Reed, and Jenna next to Rourke. They had all been separated from their partners, and from their friends, and it was fine. It made for a more interesting evening. She felt content, sitting here with people who had been strangers to her not so long ago but were now firm friends. More than anything, she felt she belonged here in Starling Bay, although home wasn't a location, it was wherever Dylan and Chloe were.

Dylan stood up suddenly. "Before we dig in and enjoy this wonderful feast that you both," he nodded at Reed and Jenna, "have put together, I have something to say."

"I had nothing to do with the putting together of the feast," confessed Jenna. "This is all Cecile's masterpiece."

"What did you want to say?" Reed asked.

"We've fixed a date for the wedding."

A murmur echoed around the table.

"We're getting married two days before Christmas."

Merry smiled, because Dylan saying their wedding date out loud seemed to make it cast in stone.

"Which Christmas?" Rourke asked.

"This Christmas," Dylan replied.

"*This*, as in … *two months' time*?" Rourke hollered.

"You said it would be next year?" Reed asked.

"We changed the date and moved it closer," said Dylan. "It's this Christmas."

"So soon?" Leigh and Jenna turned to Merry, craning their necks, their eyes wide.

"We just decided," said Merry, shrugging. "No point in waiting. If we both want to get married, there's no reason to delay things."

"Well, congratulations again," said Reed, and another toast and raising of glasses followed. Their friends digested the news.

"We don't have much time," said Jenna.

"That's only weeks away," Leigh said.

"Months," Merry replied.

"Eight weeks," Jenna clarified.

Merry experienced butterflies furiously flapping their wings in her stomach. Eight weeks didn't seem like long at all.

"We've got *plenty* of time," said Dylan calmly.

"We don't have a lot to do," Merry added. "Neither of us wants a big wedding."

"We want it small," said Dylan, his eyes never leaving her face.

"With close friends and family." That was the most important thing, Merry had decided.

"Dude!" Rourke bellowed. "One heck of a way to get out of doing the Christmas pageant."

Reed nodded. "I didn't think of that. Hyacinth's going to be devastated when she finds out."

Merry smiled at Dylan.

"It was Hyacinth's idea," he declared. Then he told them what had happened that day in the town square.

"You let Hyacinth Fitzsimmons pick your wedding date?" Reed laughed.

"That wasn't quite what happened," Merry replied, feeling defensive.

"But we got thinking," said Dylan, "And we decided it wasn't such a bad idea."

"You'd do anything to get out of the pageant," Rourke repeated.

"I can't think of a nicer way of getting out of it." Dylan smiled at her.

CHAPTER 9

"*D*awn's little brother is *so* cute," said Chloe, yawning as she stretched out on the sofa. Merry and Dylan had picked her up from her friend's house earlier. Her daughter looked tired and disheveled, and she proudly announced that they had gotten one hour's sleep.

Merry decided to let her have a lazy Sunday, and to get fully recharged before school tomorrow.

"She's got a little brother?" Merry asked, curious to know.

"James. He's five."

"It's just the two of them?"

Chloe nodded, then yawned again. "He's *so* cute, Mom."

"That's nice. How does Dawn get along with him?"

Her daughter looked at her as if she didn't understand the question. "You think he's cute," said Merry, "but sometimes, siblings can be annoying, especially a younger one. But that's part of growing up in a family, learning to get along with your brothers and sisters."

"How do you know? You don't have any brothers or sisters," Chloe pointed out.

That stunned Merry into silence. "No, I don't."

55

"And neither does Dylan."

"That's right, we're a family of only children," said Merry. "Does that bother you?"

"No, why?"

"Because you're an only child." She wanted to ask her daughter how she would feel about another addition to the family, but decided that it wasn't the right time.

"I'm used to it, and I've got Spart."

"You do have Spart." She ruffled Chloe's hair.

"Mom!" Her daughter smoothed her hair down.

"What? You're not going anywhere."

"I don't like my hair all messed up. I'm not a child," her daughter insisted. That told her. Merry moved her hand back to her lap.

"No, you're not. You've grown up so fast. *Too* fast," she murmured under her breath.

"She got bored with him."

"Who did?"

"Dawn. Are you even listening to me?"

She frowned. "Of course I'm listening."

Her daughter was indeed growing up frighteningly fast. In a few years' time, they would be talking about boyfriends, and then college, and … Merry didn't want to think about it. It was too much change to consider, especially now when she was on the brink of starting a new chapter of her life.

Merry looked at her. "Dawn got bored with?"

"With her brother. He wanted to hold her hand when we went trick or treating, but Dawn wanted to be with her friends."

"I can see why your friend got annoyed. Then what happened?"

"So his mom held his hand but he didn't want that. He wanted to be in the group with his sister." Chloe rolled her eyes. "Dawn was so mad at him."

"Little brothers or sisters can be like that, I suppose." She waited for the gap in conversation, for the space inside the silence where she could say something about Chloe possibly having a sibling one day.

But her daughter spoke first. "Did you have fun, Mom? Did everyone like your costume?"

"We had fun. It was a good night." She told Chloe what the others were dressed as at the dinner party. "We told everyone about our wedding date."

Chloe yawned.

"They were surprised it was so soon," continued Merry.

Chloe yawned again.

"Do you think it's too soon?" Merry asked.

"For what?"

"For us to be getting married." Not that she needed validation from a teenager.

"No. It's not soon, Mom."

Time obviously ran much more slowly in the world of youngsters.

"Jenna and Leigh want to help with the wedding preparations." Chloe yawned, and it made Merry yawn too. Clearly, her daughter was too tired to show any interest in the wedding. "You get some rest," she said, getting up. "I'd better break the news to Grandma."

"This means we can all be together on Christmas morning," said Chloe as Merry walked away.

"What?" Merry turned around.

"You, me, Dylan, and Spart. We'll all wake up together on Christmas morning and open the presents underneath the tree. Like real families do."

Merry blinked. "Sure, honey." She nodded. "That's exactly what we'll do. Go to sleep now, honey."

She called and announced the new date to her parents. Her father was fine, but her mother had doubts.

"*December, Meredith?*"

This was the conversation she had been dreading. "Yes, Mom."

"But why the rush? You know how much you hate—"

"That's in the past now, and I'm trying to move on." *So, please let me.* She could hear her father mumbling something in the background.

"But what about…you know?"

She held in her breath, and knew perfectly well that her mother was hinting at the anniversary of Brian's death. She and Dylan were planning to get married two months later. Not on the actual date. It wasn't disrespectful, was it?

"Mom, I only called to let you know."

Her father suddenly came back on the phone. "We're delighted for you, Meredith."

She wasn't so sure. "I know you are, Dad, but mom…"

"She's just fretting for no reason. Dylan's a wonderful man, wonderful! Not just for you, but with Chloe. I've seen how he is with her. I couldn't be happier for you all."

"Thanks, Dad." She felt a warmth radiate through her heart, easing the earlier tightness.

"Don't worry about your mother. You know what she's like."

Merry could hear her mother trying to say something in the background, and she couldn't help but smile.

"I just wanted to let you know, Dad. Explain to mom when she's calmed down."

"Don't you worry about your mother. She's happy, she just can't find the right words to articulate how she really feels right now."

Merry smiled to herself, then hung up.

Her parents had always been like this. They balanced one

another out. Her father was always the wise, patient one, always seeing the good in everything, while her mother was always prone to judge and worried for no reason.

She wondered if she and Dylan would be like this, each of them set in their own ways as they grew older.

But it was done. The announcements were made to the people closest to them.

~

It was happening.

The venues they wanted were available.

Their wedding was going ahead this side of Christmas.

"December?" Laura asked, expressing mild surprise when Dylan told her.

"We don't want to wait until next year."

Instead of having a wedding hanging over his head—and hanging was the wrong word for it because their wedding wasn't an axe. It was something he couldn't wait for. A Christmas wedding meant a new start for a new year. He liked the sound of that.

"Merry and I are planning to go away for a vacation, soon after Christmas day." He looked at Laura, hoping to catch her reaction. She hadn't asked for any more time off aside from the week leading up to Christmas. While he wasn't expecting her to hold the fort in their absence, he needed her to be available in case something went wrong.

"I should be fine to come in," Laura told him.

"You don't need to tell me right away. I expect you haven't finalized your plans yet, but Chloe's parents will be here. They've offered to help, though, of course, they don't know about the workings of this place as well as you do."

The good thing was that Merry's parents had offered to help

out. They would stay and take care of Chloe, and so it worked out well.

Chloe helped out at the store sometimes, and knew about its workings. Merry's parents and Chloe taking care of it would set his mind at ease, and if Laura could come in too, he wouldn't have to worry about the store at all while they were on their honeymoon.

"Dylan, stop worrying. The store will be fine."

He only worried because Christmas time in Starling Bay was one of the busiest.

Hyacinth's drive to push the town as a go-to place for Christmas vacation had worked. The Christmas markets and the bustling, merry town square would be decked out in Christmas decorations in a few weeks' time.

"I don't doubt you," he said quickly.

"I should be fine to keep an eye on it, especially if I have your in-laws helping me."

"Thanks." That was all he'd needed to know. "I'll be in the workshop all day."

"Slaving over the vases, no doubt," replied Laura.

"They sell well."

"I'd noticed."

He headed towards his workshop.

If he was going to be gone over Christmas, he had to make sure everything was done well in advance, all the vases and products he sold in the store had to be made so that there was no shortfall while he and Merry were away.

CHAPTER 10

"What do you think?" Leigh asked. She offered Merry a third slice of cake from a different plate.

Merry took a bite of the rich, moist, buttery cake. It was nutty, but she couldn't tell what type of nut it was. "Oh my goodness, that's divine," she cried. The cake melted in her mouth.

"I knew you would like it."

"What is it?"

"Pistachio and apricot."

Merry's eyes flew wide open. "How do you put all these flavors together and make each and every one of them taste so scrumptious?"

Leigh shrugged. "I've always loved baking, and the internet is a good place for finding recipes."

"They're all good." She took a sip of tea, then forked up another mouthful of cake. "I love this. I really, *really* love this. I love them all, but if I had to go for one, which I do, since I'm only allowed one wedding cake, it's this one."

Leigh had made three cakes for her. An orange blossom and honey cake, an apple and cinnamon layer cake and a pistachio and apricot cake.

Each of them were divine.

"I'll have an alternative for anyone who can't eat nuts," said Leigh.

"That's a good idea." Merry wiped her mouth. "Could I take some for Dylan? I feel he needs to make this decision with me. Even though," she lowered her voice to a whisper, "the decision has already been made."

"I've packed you three containers. There's some for Chloe as well."

"You're so sweet." She was genuinely touched. "I didn't expect you to bake three cakes for me to try out." This would have eaten up a huge chunk of Leigh's time and effort, and Leigh had enough going on what with running her bookshop.

"It's not a problem, really. I love baking, and I wanted to help."

"Well, it's very sweet of you. Thank you." The friendships she had made here over the course of the year were priceless. She felt as if she'd known Leigh and Jenna for years. "And don't forget, Jenna say's we're going shopping for a dress this weekend."

"I've put the day aside." Leigh told her. "Are you excited?"

"To be honest, I haven't had much time to think about it. Neither has Dylan. Things are so hectic. He's so busy, and so am I. It's only in the evenings that we sit down and discuss the wedding."

"You're trying to squeeze into a few months what most people spend a year or more doing."

"Maybe." Merry looked at her watch. "I should get back to the store. I've taken too much of your time."

"No, you haven't." Leigh got up and put the three plastic containers into a bag. "See what Dylan and Chloe think. Let me know what you decide on, and also for how many people."

Merry took one final sip of her almost-finished tea and

finished off the last remaining piece of cake. "We're looking at around fifty people at the most, but I'll confirm soon."

"See you on Saturday," said Leigh as they kissed each other on the cheek.

"What's happening on Saturday?"

Leigh gave her an amused look. "We're looking for your wedding dress, remember?"

"My wedding dress. How could I forget?"

"What in the world…?" Dylan examined the vase in shock. It was still soft. He checked the others, and they were the same. For some reason, the kiln hadn't fired properly, and it seemed as if it hadn't reached the right temperature.

Darn it.

This was the last thing he needed.

He reached into the kiln again, and heard the sound of footsteps behind him. With a huge disappointed sigh, he set yet another the floppy vase onto his worktop.

"I have some cake for you. I have lots of cake, actually." Merry looked at him, then at the vases on the worktop, then stopped. "What's wrong?"

"There's a problem with the kiln. It's not reaching the right temperature." If this didn't get fixed in the next day or so, he was going to have problems.

"Can you rebake them?" she asked.

He heaved out a sigh. "It's called 'firing'."

"I'm sorry. I'm not a potter."

He immediately regretted his sarcastic reply. "Sorry, I'm just annoyed. It's a problem I don't need right now, or ever." But it wasn't a problem he needed right now during his busy season, and with the wedding moving alarmingly closer. These past few weeks, he and Merry had made a concerted effort to focus on the business so that they would have less to worry about as their wedding day approached.

For him, this meant building up his inventory of goods. For her, it meant racing on ahead with the tasks at the department store, but also becoming aggressive with her Christmas marketing for the gift store.

She walked over to him and placed her palm against the back of his neck; it was a comforting gesture. "Don't worry," she said, her voice soothing him. "It can be fixed, though, can't it? You can call someone out?"

"I can. I've got the number in my office." He walked away to get it, and when he returned, Merry was still waiting for him. "What?" he asked her.

"You look so stressed. It's not the end of the world."

"I have a large order for the vases."

"But this will get fixed soon enough, won't it?" Merry asked. He hoped so but even a day's delay was going to set him back. "I don't want to fall behind on the vase order."

"Then you'll just have to work through the night. I'll stay up with you, because we have lots to do now."

With the wedding just over a month away, and Christmas making life busier and more hectic than usual, things had suddenly sped up.

"Thanks." He loved that she was a part of his life, because she made everything better. "Is it me or has time sped up ever since we fixed our wedding date?"

"Time has definitely sped up. Everything is turning insanely hectic. Even at the store." She groaned.

"Then cut back on your hours here at the store."

She spluttered in surprise. "No way. This here is your business. You're the one who's spent years building it up."

"It's our business now, and you've turned it around ever since you've been here, but if you want to keep the job at the department store, you can't slack off there too much."

"Who's slacking off?" she asked, visibly startled.

He let out a grunt. He was taking his frustrations out on Merry, and he hadn't intended to. "I'm sorry. I'm not in the best of moods right now. You're not a slacker."

"And I would much rather work harder at *our* business. Besides, I like working here because I get to stare at my hunky boss all day long."

"Hunky boss?" He let the words sink in and smiled. "I like that."

"I'm taking my laptop on our honeymoon with me," she warned him.

She had to be joking. "On our honeymoon?"

"I need to keep track of the advertising, set the budget, see how much we're spending daily."

Nevertheless, this wasn't allowed. It had to be illegal. "But on our *honeymoon?*"

She kissed his chin. "It will take ten minutes out of my day. You can spare me ten minutes to keep an eye on the business, can't you?"

"Rather it be you than me." He kissed her on her nose. "Only ten minutes."

From that one decision to propose sooner than he had intended, everything seemed to be hurtling along at breakneck speed. It was as if their wedding had taken on a life of its own, the timing and the speed of it, like a chain of dominos had started moving from the moment he'd taken Merry for a surprise walk in the woods. He was happy, and he was glad that things were happening this fast, and seemingly of their own accord.

"I need to review our advertising strategy," said Merry, stretching out her arms. "When you've called the kiln people, come over to the kitchen. I've got some of Leigh's cake and coffee, and then we'll both get back to work." She got up and walked towards the door when someone knocked. Merry opened it.

"Leah Shriver's here," Laura told them. "She said she wanted to speak to you, Dylan."

He felt the insides of his gut tighten. What did she want?

"Leah Shriver?" asked Merry, looking at him.

"Come with me." He reached for her hand and walked through into the store, with Merry close behind him.

Leah stood at the counter, her arms folded, her smile fixed.

"I hear congratulations are in order," she said, miserably, eyeing Merry as if she were about to corner her. The women smiled at one another, before Leah continued, "Hyacinth told me you won't be around to direct the Christmas pageant."

"Good news does travel fast," said Dylan rather enthusiastically. "We're getting married the day before."

"Such perfect timing."

He squeezed Merry's hand gently. "Purely coincidental."

"Congratulations." But the word sounded cold, as if Leah had just said 'commiserations.'

He thanked her anyway.

"Hyacinth's put me in charge of the Christmas pageant," she announced. The news instantly cheered him up.

"That's an excellent idea! You would be perfect for the role."

"You really think so?" Leah asked him.

"You've been there right by my side for all the previous shows. You know how it's run. You know everything."

"Good luck," said Merry. It was the first time she had spoken.

"And good luck to you. A new move, a wedding. Whatever next?" The way Leah said it, it sounded more like an insult than a blessing. He could tell by Merry's stunned silence that she too was surprised by this response.

"Is there anything I can help you with?" Dylan asked.

"Do you have any tips? Could you maybe show up at the first rehearsal?" she asked jokingly, and it was hard for him to tell if she was really joking or being serious.

"For what?" And no, he couldn't. This time it was Merry who squeezed his hand.

"Just for courage. I'm a little nervous."

"I can't. I'm busy, but you'll be fine. You're a pro at this. You were my right-hand woman." He regretted that choice of words.

"I suppose I just have to get on with it," said Leah. "Good luck with the wedding."

They both thanked her, and he waited with bated breath to hear if she had another catty remark to make. Thankfully, she left without saying anything more.

"That woman has a crush on you," Merry said as soon as the coast was clear.

"I've never thought of her in that way."

She hugged him from behind. "I know. I remember last year at rehearsal time."

He sighed loudly. "Thank goodness you're here."

They stayed that way for a few seconds, before he forced himself to move away. "I need to call the kiln people and pray that they can fix it right away."

CHAPTER 11

She stared at her laptop in horror.

Almost $3,000 had been charged on their business credit card, and it was for purchases that neither she nor Dylan had made.

They had been hacked.

Victims of credit card fraud.

She had just received a text alert from her bank as she had been putting in croissants to bake, and she had rushed to her laptop to check.

"Mom!"

"What is it?" Merry called from the bedroom. This was supposed to be a joyous day of shopping for wedding dresses with her friends, but it had already turned into a nightmare.

"The timer's ringing," Chloe wailed.

The croissants were ready.

Sighing, Merry placed her laptop on the bed, and rushed out towards the kitchen.

On the weekends she made chocolate croissants for breakfast. Not from scratch, only the ready-to-bake ones. She was no Leigh with her super-ninja baking skills.

Three thousand dollars.

The shock of it overwhelmed her, and she couldn't get the dollar amount out of her head. Dylan would have a heart attack when she told him, and she didn't want to worry him because the man was already stressed enough.

She opened the oven, then pulled out the baking tray, then screamed as a sharp pain sliced through her fingers.

The tray dropped, clattering like a dustbin lid skittering across the hard kitchen floor.

"Mom!" Chloe came running as Merry breathed through the pain. Her fingertips felt as if they were on fire. "Quick, Mom! Put them under cold water."

"Spart, NO!" Merry cried, as Spartacus tried to chomp away on the croissants which had scattered all over the floor. She pushed him away. "No, Spart!" she cried in anger. "Naughty boy!" Chocolate was a big no-no. She pushed him out of the kitchen, because the last thing she needed was to take him to the vet's.

"What in the world happened here?" Dylan stood at the kitchen door, looking concerned.

"Mom burned herself," explained Chloe, as she frantically tried to sweep up the mess on the floor. "Mom, put your fingers under the faucet."

Merry had been so worried about Spartacus eating chocolate that she hadn't yet managed to put her fingers under cold running water, despite her pain.

Dylan stepped forward and helped Merry over to the sink, forcing her fingers under the cold water.

"Better?" he asked, turning the faucet to maximum capacity.

"Better," she said, breathing out slowly. The cold water dulled the pain.

"What happened?"

"I forgot to put on my oven mitts." She glanced over her shoulder to find Chloe on the floor, cleaning up the mess.

"Thanks, honey. We've got some more croissants in the fridge, if you want to put them in."

"Don't you worry about breakfast. Come and sit down," Dylan told her. She did as she was told, partly because her fingers felt as if they'd been sliced by a heated knife, and partly because of the shock of the fraudulent transactions. "I'll sort out breakfast," said Dylan. He looked around for her first aid kit.

"I'll be fine," she said, moving her fingers away. They were starting to swell.

"You'll be even better after this." He got out a tube of ointment.

"I'm supposed to go shopping for wedding dresses."

"You are still going shopping for dresses. I'll take care of Chloe. You go." He rubbed ointment on her fingers, then put a bandage over them. "How come you forgot the oven mitts?"

She didn't want to talk about money in front of Chloe. She looked at Dylan, and shook her head.

He looked even more worried now. "Are you having second thoughts?"

"About what?"

"The wedding."

"That's what you concluded from me burning my fingers? Don't ever turn into a private investigator."

He laughed. "You're shopping for wedding dresses. It's a natural conclusion."

"It is not!"

"Don't go flaking out on me," he said with a grin. "That's all I'm saying."

That's what he was worried about? She rushed to reassure him. "As if I would." But the question still remained of how she was going to tell him about the money. She also needed to call the bank and put a stop to the card.

"I'll take care of that, Chloe," Dylan said to her daughter. "You go and get ready, because we're going to have breakfast at Roxy's Diner."

Chloe whooped for joy. "Really?"

"Yes, really."

Chloe rushed out of the kitchen. "That's nice of you," Merry said.

"If you're going shopping at Whisper Falls, Chloe and I can treat ourselves to breakfast at Roxy's. It's only fair."

She checked to make sure that her daughter had left, then broke the news to him. "Someone spent $3,000 on our business credit card."

Dylan stared at her as if she'd spoken in Russian. "Someone did what?" He blinked, his facial expression turning to one of shock.

"Someone spent $3,000 of our money. Overnight." She winced as she said it.

"Three thousand dollars?"

"They're all fraudulent purchases. Nothing we've bought. I was checking the account when I rushed out to check on the croissants." She tried to stand up, pressed her hand on the chair, then gasped in pain.

"Careful," he told her.

"I need to call the bank and put a stop on the card. That's what I was about to do when the oven timer went off."

"The bank will reverse the charges," he told her. He seemed to be handling the news better than she had. She hated being a victim of fraud. Hated that someone had spent their hard-earned money. It was invasive; like someone reaching inside her purse with their dirty fingers and taking everything in it.

He must have seen how upset she was because he lowered his

head so that his face was only inches from hers. His cologne swept over her, and instantly, she felt better. "It's only money, Merry. We'll get it back."

"I know we will." She knew it wouldn't impact them too much because the bank would take care of it, but still, it was an irritating and annoying problem to have. It killed her mood to go shopping with the girls.

"Hey," he said. "We'll get reimbursed. Stop looking so worried."

He was right, of course. But she wasn't sure about going to Whisper Falls. "I'm going to call Jenna and ask her to postpone our trip."

"We don't have long, Merry. You're not going to buy a dress in the one or two weeks before the big day, are you?"

Once again, he was right.

"Okay, okay," she said. Her excitement had long fizzled out, and her fingers hurt, and she was worried about the money. But he was right. She didn't have long. No matter what, she had to go shopping today.

"Spart's okay," said Chloe, reappearing. She looked at her mother's hands, turning them over gently in hers. "Do they hurt a lot?"

Merry tried to be brave. "Only a little bit."

"Are you ready to go?" She looked at her daughter's black leggings, and her oversized sweatshirt and tried to disguise her disapproval. She was suddenly haunted by a yearning for the days when she used to dress Chloe. When she used to pick out lovely little dresses, or matching, coordinated pants and tops and skirts. Now her teen daughter preferred to live in oversized clothing, and Merry didn't like the style at all.

"We need to go shopping and get you something, sweetie. Find you a nice dress to wear on the wedding day."

"Does it have to be a *dress?*" Chloe asked, wrinkling up her nose as if the mention of the word was painful.

Merry was determined that on that day, her daughter would wear something lovely and girly. "Do you think you could for the one day, for my sake?"

"Can I pick the color?"

"Pink or pale yellow, take your pick."

Chloe put her finger in her mouth and made a retching motion. "Mom," she whined. "I haven't worn those color dresses since kindergarten."

"And how much I miss those days." Merry smiled at the memories.

"All done," said Dylan, returning to the kitchen. "Ready to leave?"

"Not yet. I'm going to call the bank first. You go on. I'll call Jenna and tell her to meet me in the parking lot. She was going to drive us there. Just as well, since I don't think I can."

Luckily, Jenna also lived in Forest Heights and was only a short walking distance away from Merry. She'd lost all her enthusiasm for the shopping trip, but the thought of spending the entire day with her friends brought a smile to her lips.

A few hours later, she, Jenna and Leigh were in Whisper Falls at the wedding dress shop Jenna had told her about.

On the way here, they had also stopped off at a couple of department stores and designer shops to have a look, but Merry hadn't liked the designer price tags and didn't have an eye for designer tastes.

Always, at the back of her mind was the fact that she didn't need a big, flashy wedding.

Nevertheless, she tried on eight dresses. It would have been just three, but having Jenna and Leigh accompanying her meant that she had to occasionally pander to both their suggestions.

She tried all different styles; a meringue one with puffed sleeves, one that was tight all over, one that was lacy and had a plunging neckline, another lacy one that was far too revealing for a wedding dress—off the shoulder and with almost no back—and she wondered how the thing would hold up.

She picked one she really liked and tried it on, then walked back out to the main showroom to show her friends. It was simple, with no sequins, and light beadwork.

"It's too plain," said Jenna, shaking her head. "That's the type of dress I could make at home on a budget, if I had no money and if I was getting married."

Merry's jaw almost hit the floor. "You don't hold back, do you? I happen to like this one."

Leigh was nicer and kinder. "It's not *too* bad. You can accessorize it."

"I like it. I like it because it's not frilly or too over the top."

"It's your wedding," Jenna reminded her. "You're supposed to be slightly over the top on your big day. You're the star attraction, not the side show."

They didn't understand it. They wouldn't. She was excited, and couldn't wait to become Mrs. Dylan Fraser. The allure of the big day was great, but it was nothing compared to the rest of it; taking vows that would bind her and Dylan together forever. This time around, she deeply understood what they meant. When she had first gotten married, she had been younger, more carefree, blissfully ignorant of the curveballs life could throw.

That wedding day had been all about the big day, the cake, the dress, the flowers, the food. The honeymoon. Now that she was older and wiser, it had a different connotation for her. This time around it was the strength of commitment, the lasting bond, the reassurance of never being lonely and the comfort of being a couple—these were the things she sought.

How could she explain to her friends in a way that didn't make it sound as if she was preaching?

"I've been the star attraction before. I'm happy to be dignified and understated now. I don't want to be the center of attention."

"But Dylan hasn't had a wedding day before," Leigh chimed in. "And Rourke tells me he's going all out."

Jenna nodded in agreement. "Reed says the guy never used to talk about settling down. Meeting you was a huge turnaround for him."

That stopped her. She smoothed her Band-Aided fingers over her plain wedding dress. Dylan was excited—and so was she—but she wasn't, for some reason, feeling it. "Fine. Maybe I will try on something a little more… sparkly." She didn't like the idea of it, but if Dylan was going to look so darned gorgeous on the day, she had to look her absolute best. She would, of that she was sure, but the day had started off in a mess, and she still couldn't get her head around the idea of excitement.

Jenna flashed her a wide smile, and it immediately made Merry suspicious. "I saw you looking at this earlier, then you put it back on the rack. But we like it. We think you should try it."

She held up a dress. It looked expensive, made from lovely silky material, and intricate embroidery and beading. Merry recalled looking at it on the rack before dismissing it. The neckline seemed too low for her taste. "Fine," she said, taking it from her friend.

"Fine," said her friends in unison.

She changed into the new dress, and when she couldn't do up the buttons along the back, she called one of the shop assistants in to help her. When the assistant had finished helping her, Merry turned around and stared in the mirror.

"It's a little too fitted," she said, peering at herself in the mirror. The bodice pushed up her breasts a little too much, and the dress skimmed her hips a little too tightly, but, goodness, she looked… amazing.

She *felt* amazing.

The assistant clasped her hands together. "You look beautiful." The look on the assistant's face mirrored exactly how Merry felt about the dress when she looked at her reflection in the mirror. It did look beautiful on her, and she did look stunning. Her mood lifted in an instant.

"Thank you." Merry's heart started to beat faster. Suddenly, she no longer cared that it emphasized her chest, or that it felt a little tighter. She loved it. It had the right amount of beading, and made the plain dress she had tried on earlier look totally inferior.

She walked out of the fitting rooms, and saw Jenna and Leigh's mouths fall open.

Jenna blinked.

Leigh stopped eating the bar of chocolate she had in her hands. "Oh, Merry," she gasped.

"Oh, honey." Jenna's eyes turned round. "*This* is it."

"I know, right?" Merry was so overwhelmed and felt almost close to tears. There was no doubting the fact, *this* was the dress.

"Turn around," Jenna urged. "Give us a whirl."

Merry obliged, and spun around, feeling like a fairytale princess.

"That's the one," Leigh announced.

"I knew it would be." Merry agreed happily.

"But you put it back on the rack," challenged Jenna.

"Then I'm lucky to have friends like you who forced me into it."

"Does it fit properly all over?" the shop assistant asked.

Merry looked at herself in the huge ornate mirror that hung outside in the fitting rooms. She smoothed her hands down, being careful not to touch the silky fabric in case she snagged it.

"It fits perfectly all over." They got up and stood by her, examining it closely.

"It's like it was made for you." Jenna smoothed her hand over the back. "These buttons are cute. Such lovely detail."

"You have to get this, Merry" Leigh begged.

"I'm going to. I might ask for some alterations," she said to the shop assistant. Have it adjusted so that it wasn't too tight along her hips.

"We can certainly do that for you. You'll just need to put down a deposit for the dress."

"That's fine. And you'll have it ready in time? We're getting married two days before Christmas."

"How lovely! We'll have it ready on time. Don't worry."

CHAPTER 12

"What did you think of Whisper Falls?" he asked. It was a beautiful little town about an hour's drive from Starling Bay, but there were plenty of other shops and stores along the way.

"It's pretty." Merry took another forkful of pistachio cake. She'd come back late, because they had gone over to Jenna's place and had take-out. Dylan had cooked for himself and Chloe, and they'd watched a movie on TV before Chloe went to bed.

"It is pretty. Why all the way there? I mean," he backtracked, not wanting to sound negative about anything regarding the wedding, "It seems like a long way to go, though I guess nowhere is too far if you're looking at wedding dresses."

"I didn't drive." Merry held up her fingers. "Jenna took us. She said they had a lovely wedding dress shop there, and she was right. Have you ever been?"

"To Whisper Falls? Once."

"I found the perfect dress, but I'm concerned it might be a little tight fitting."

"In one trip?" This was surprising. He'd heard that it took

women weeks, if not months, to set their hearts on the perfect dress.

"I had to try on eight of them first."

"Only eight?" He ran his fingers gently over Merry's bandaged fingers, wincing because they looked so bad. "Does that hurt?"

She shook her head. "Surprisingly, no, not any more. I had one of the best first-aiders taking care of me."

He smiled. "Obviously." But he wanted to know more about the wedding dress. "You only tried on eight dresses?"

"It would have been three, but Jenna and Leigh, they had their own ideas."

"Jenna can be particularly persuasive."

"There was one I really liked, but they both hated it the most."

"Why?"

"They said it was too plain and simple."

"Nothing wrong with plain and simple," he remarked.

"That's what I said."

"Seems to be that you and I have similar ideas."

"That's why we're such a great team." She leaned across the table, squeezed his hand. "Ouch. Now it hurts."

He lifted her hand and kissed it gently. "You're not going to tell me about the dress, are you?"

"You can tell me what you think of it when you see me on our big day."

It seemed awful late to be having cake, but Merry reminded him that it was never too late to eat cake. The delicious samples Leigh had given them had all been huge, thankfully, and days later they were still happily eating them.

"Have we decided?" Merry asked. They sat across the kitchen table from one another, finishing off what was left of the cake samples Leigh had given.

Talk about making impossible decisions. "Hard to decide

when it comes to Leigh and her baking." He'd liked them all, but he had to agree, the pistachio cake was the clear winner.

"She's super talented," Merry agreed.

"Rourke's going to have to watch his waistline."

Merry laughed. "I'm going to have to watch mine if I'm going to get into the wedding dress. It's already tight enough."

His eyes lit up. "Tight fitting?"

"I've asked for some alterations to be made. It's a little too figure hugging for me."

He sighed, raking his hand through his hair as the image of Merry dressed as Morticia came to his mind. "You'll look gorgeous no matter what you're wearing. I will love you in anything, even in a potato sack."

"You'll love me in this dress more, I promise. It might sound like I'm boasting, but even I couldn't stop looking at myself in the mirror." She grinned at him cheekily.

"That good, huh?" Because Merry wasn't one to admire herself in the mirror like that.

He liked that Jenna and Leigh were helping her with the wedding preparations, Leigh with the cake side of things, and Jenna telling Merry about where to shop for wedding dresses, because Merry wouldn't have known, being new to the area. As for himself, he had never paid any attention to things related to weddings, so these acts of kindness from her friends were comforting and helpful.

"Shall I tell Leigh that we've decided on this?" Merry asked, sliding a piece of the cake on her fork into his mouth.

"I like the pistachio one."

"Good, then it's settled. Though I'd hinted that it probably would be the one we'd decide on. I'll tell her, and I'll pay her for it upfront."

"I doubt she'll accept it." He knew Rourke and Leigh wouldn't accept money for it. But Dylan was a man of principle, and he wanted to pay his way. Merry would want to do the same. As things stood, Reed had already helped him get a good rate for one of the banquet rooms at The Grand Hotel, where they had decided to have their reception after the church wedding.

Next week, the guys were taking him to the department store to get his wedding tux. All that now remained was the honeymoon and he had almost gotten that booked. Merry hated flying, and so he had to find a somewhere that wasn't going to take an entire day to drive to.

"She'll have to. I can't have her do this for us at no cost. How was your day?" she asked.

"We had fun. No dresses were tried on, though."

"Funny. Though I need to take Chloe shopping. I've threatened her with a yellow or pink dress to wear on the day."

He frowned. "Yellow or pink? This is Chloe you're talking about? Good luck with that."

"I'm getting married, and this time around she gets to be at the wedding. She has to do as I say."

"I'm sure she will." He imagined Chloe not liking it, but he felt she would, given the occasion.

"How was breakfast?"

"Great. Roxy's place is all done up and looking Christmassy. We were content to just sit there for a while."

"I remember when I discovered it last year, it was soon after we got here. I loved Roxy's Diner. I peered through the windows and saw all the decorations, and I couldn't *not* go in. What did you do after that?"

"We wandered around the town square. Chloe's class are doing a Secret Santa at school, and she wanted to get something for that as well as buy a few things for her friends."

"Who does she have to get the Secret Santa gift for?"

He chuckled. "A boy, and it completely threw her."

"What did she buy?"

"A book."

Merry laughed. "That's not the right kind of present for a boy."

"I loved reading when I was a child," he protested. It had been a favorite pastime of his. He would lose himself in the worlds of *The Three Musketeers* and *Robinson Crusoe*.

"But you're one of a kind, Mr. Fraser."

"I'm glad you think so." He picked up his coffee cup and took a sip.

"I think so enough to marry you, before someone else snatched you up."

"Wasn't nobody else in sight to snatch me up."

"That's not what I heard," protested Merry.

He was curious to discover. "What did you hear? And from whom?"

"From the girls. There's something I like about me being best friends with your best friends' girlfriends."

"There's no such thing as secrets, then," he remarked.

"Leah Shriver is a name which comes to mind."

"As you are well aware, that attraction was purely one-way," he replied.

"I wonder how she's doing with the pageant."

"I don't know, and I don't care. Add pageant to the list of words we're not allowed to use in the house."

"Very funny. Oh," she jolted, as if she'd remembered something. "I put a stop on the card, but I need to attach a new one to our advertising account otherwise our ads will stop running." She started to get up, but he grabbed her by the arm.

"Don't worry about that now. You can do that later."

"I might forget."

"Stay," he said. "I haven't seen you all day."

"Let me change it and I'll be back."

"You only just got home. Stay. Don't you want to hear about the rest of our day?"

She relented, but this time perched herself on his lap, a move which sent sparks scattering across his body.

"That's better." He instinctively put his arm around her waist, and nuzzled his face against her neck. The mere scent of her perfume and the warmth of her skin always set his pulse racing.

"What's happening with the kiln?" she asked, bringing him back to planet Earth.

He sighed. The kiln was going to ruin his monthly sales if he wasn't careful. "Someone's coming to fix it next week."

"*Next week*?" Merry looked horrified. "Can't they come sooner?"

"Apparently not." He had pleaded with the support guy, telling him that he was getting married soon, and had a huge order he needed to get ready to deliver but the guy was fully booked and couldn't accommodate him.

"Will you still be able to fulfil the order for the vases?"

"Yes." He would do whatever it took. But this was November's order. He hoped the order for December would be less.

"You poor thing." She pressed her lips against his.

"That makes it all better," he murmured.

"It does?" she asked, a sultry tone creeping into her voice.

He nodded his head, and she moved in for another kiss.

CHAPTER 13

The call came first thing in the morning just as she was about to go into a meeting with the marketing manager. At first she had no idea who it was from.

"Ms. Nicholls?"

"Yes?"

"This is Eloise from the wedding dress shop. You visited us over the weekend?"

"Which wedding dress shop?" They had visited a fair number of shops.

"In Whisper Falls."

"Oh, yes. That's right." She cheered up at the thought of it.

"I wasn't here that day. I was at a wedding, unfortunately, but I am sorry to tell you that there has been a terrible mistake."

Merry frowned. One of her work colleagues walked past her and into the meeting room, tapping her finger on her wristwatch to signal to Merry that the meeting was about to start. "What sort of mistake?"

"I'm afraid the dress you paid the deposit for wasn't for sale."

Merry spluttered, trying to think back and determine what was going on. "It was for sale. I tried it on," she protested. "It had a price tag on it. And your assistant took my measurements in order to make adjustments."

"I'm so sorry, Ms. Nicholls. It should not have been up for sale. It should have been put away. The dress was already paid for in full by someone earlier that day. There's been an error of momentous proportions. I am so sorry."

Merry's mouth fell open. "But I love that dress. It's perfect. It's *my* dress." She didn't mean to sound so petulant, but she couldn't help it.

"I'm so sorry, Ms. Nicholls. I can't tell you what an awful, *awful* mistake this has been and I apologize profusely."

"But, but..." She ran out of words. This was devastating. She had never expected to feel so upset over a dress, even a wedding dress, but this bad news had rammed into her like a freight train.

Her friend stuck her head around the door. "Hurry up," she hissed. "We're all waiting for you."

Merry let out a groan. She had to go, but this wasn't the last of it. "I'm about to go into a meeting," she told the wedding dress shop owner. "I don't know what you expect me to do. I had set my heart on that dress. That's the dress I intend to wear at my wedding."

"I'm so sorry, Ms. Nicholls. We only sell one of kind. I can't even source you another wedding dress."

The news was as shocking as it was unexpected, and she felt as if she'd been slapped. She was about to protest again when her friend hissed at her, and Merry hung up.

It was one saga after another, and she simply didn't know how to deal with it any more.

She walked into the meeting, and tried to push the wedding dress problems out of her mind and focus, but her mind kept drifting.

Everything was going wrong.

Things had started to go wrong from the moment she and Dylan had made the decision to bring the wedding forward.

Was life trying to tell her something?

Was she rushing into things?

Outwardly, she felt she was ready to move on, but perhaps her deep-seated fears were coming to the surface and manifesting in all sorts of problems and obstacles.

As the meeting continued, she doodled on her notepad, trying to make sense of it all.

When the meeting was over, she rushed back to her desk and called the wedding dress shop manager back, but further conversation didn't resolve her problem. The woman apologized profusely all over again, but all the apologies in the world couldn't bring her dress back.

Merry was heartbroken—to her surprise, much more than she thought she would be. Ordinarily, she wasn't one to get so hung up about clothes, but this wasn't just an ordinary item of clothing. This dress signified a new start, and a new life, and a new chapter.

She'd set her heart on it, and it was perfect. She couldn't comprehend having to look for another one.

It wasn't something she wanted to burden Dylan with. With almost a month to go until the wedding, the poor guy already had enough to worry about. She called her friends and asked if they could meet her for a quick bite to eat.

They agreed to meet at Leigh's bookshop where Merry broke the awful news.

"The dress wasn't for sale *at all*?" Jenna repeated, clearly outraged.

"The lady said it shouldn't have been put out on the rack for sale in the first place. They've got new assistants, the owner was at a wedding, and there had been a mix-up."

"Sounds like the worst possible mix-up," Leigh added. "What are you going to do now?"

Merry let out a weary breath. "I have to find another dress, but, I'm not sure..." She was beginning to wonder if postponing the wedding until next year, sticking to their original plan, might be the only thing to do. Otherwise, she was in danger of buying a dress her heart wasn't set on.

Dylan was already stressed, because even if the kiln got fixed, he would still have to work like a madman to get the vases made and delivered in time.

Would it be worth the hassle to make this wedding happen given that everything was falling apart around them?

Leigh cut the quiche they were having for lunch into slices. It looked appetizing, and Jenna and Leigh dove into it with gusto but Merry had lost her appetite long before she arrived at the bookshop.

Hyacinth had made a simple mistake in assuming they were getting married at Christmas, and Merry had jumped on that mistake wanting to get married sooner, rather than leaving it until sometime next year. Dylan had been content to wait. It was her fault that they had rushed.

He was clearly accommodating her wishes, the way he always did, but with things not going according to plan, she was forced to consider the alternatives.

"Maybe we should delay the wedding?" she asked, thinking out loud.

"Delay the wedding?" her friends cried in unison.

"I've already bought my outfit," cried Jenna, before adding quickly, "But it doesn't matter. I can always wear it whenever you get married."

"Are you sure about postponing?" Leigh asked. "It seems a bit drastic."

They didn't know about the credit card fraud, and she hadn't mentioned to them about Dylan's kiln problems or about it affecting his production. "I don't know if we're rushing things," she said.

The women looked at her as if they were waiting for her to say more.

Jenna put down her cutlery. "Do what feels right for you, honey. Go with your gut."

That was the problem, up until this rash of problems, she had gone with her gut. Marrying Dylan seemed right. Marrying in such a short time span seemed perfect, but with all things going wrong, she couldn't ignore the signals.

She wasn't a superstitious person, but she was starting to wonder if life was giving her hints.

"You do whatever feels right, Merry," Leigh said. "If you don't get married in December, you'll get married later on. What's the worst that could happen?"

A laugh escaped Merry's lips. That was Dylan's expression, and it sounded serendipitous coming from Leigh's lips.

"And if you move it, then Dylan will have to do the Christmas pageant for Hyacinth." Jenna giggled, and Leigh joined in.

"She's really not so bad once you get to know her," Jenna said.

"You're still working for her," Leigh grumbled, "that says something."

"I need the work, and she offered it to me when I didn't have many options available to me."

"Not that you need the money," Leigh commented. "You could leave now if you wanted to."

"And do what?"

"I'm sure the townspeople would be more receptive to hiring you, now that you've worked for Hyacinth."

Merry gave Jenna a sympathetic smile. It was no secret between the three of them that things had turned sour for Jenna after Reed's engagement had fallen through. Wicked rumors had started up, suggesting that Jenna had been the cause of the breakup.

In a small town such as Starling Bay, rumors spread fast, but a sudden job offer from Hyacinth seemed to save the day for Jenna.

"Dylan wouldn't do the Christmas pageant," she told her friends. "Leah Shriver's taking it over."

Leigh blinked at her. Merry had told her friends about Leah's infatuation with Dylan. "She came to the store to congratulate us on our engagement."

"Really?" Jenna asked, her voice full of suspicion.

"It was slightly awkward; she still likes Dylan, I'm sure, but he's mine," she cried, exaggerating in an exaggeratedly wicked voice. "He's all mine, mine, mine."

"Then maybe you don't postpone your wedding if you want to make him yours." Jenna air-quoted the 'yours'.

"Unless you feel it's the right thing to do," added Leigh, being the voice of reason. "You have to let us know quickly."

"I will." She would speak to Dylan about it. Christmas was so busy, and the wedding two days before Christmas day would affect everyone's plans for the holidays. If she and Dylan decided to move the wedding date, they needed to make a quick decision and tell everyone as soon as possible. "Quickly?" She looked at her friends. "Why quickly?"

"No reason," said Jenna, stuffing a slice of quiche into her mouth.

Merry didn't trust them. "What are you two up to?"

"Nothing," they said again at the same time. It only made her more suspicious.

Fear settled in her belly, throwing up all sorts of wild thoughts. "What have you heard?" She wondered if Dylan had said something to Reed and Rourke that she hadn't been privy to?

"It's nothing," said Leigh with an unnatural smile.

Merry cocked her head. "Is Dylan having second thoughts?" If he was, he would be sure to tell his friends.

"You're not having second thoughts, are you?" Jenna asked, never one to miss a thing.

Merry pressed her lips together. "Not doubts, as such."

"*Not doubts, as such?*" Leigh echoed.

"You *are* having doubts?" Jenna asked, surprised. She put her hand over Merry's and squeezed it. "Honey, it's one thing postponing the wedding because you're running out of time to get everything sorted out, but it's something else if you're having doubts. What's going on?"

Merry didn't speak for a moment, and wondered if her baby talk had put Dylan off? Despite him telling her that he couldn't wait to get married, maybe he was trying not to hurt her feelings by not telling the truth? He was that kind of man. He would do anything to not hurt her, even if it was something he didn't want to do.

Leigh and Jenna exchanged those looks again. Anxiety spiked in Merry's stomach, and she was about to ask them again what they were hiding. But Jenna's phone rang and she answered it quickly.

"I'm coming," Jenna said, speaking into the phone, then glancing at Merry and Leigh. She made a face. "I popped out to get some cake. I'm coming back right now." She hung up.

"Did you just lie to Hyacinth?" Merry asked.

"Not to Hyacinth. Just another coworker."

Leigh looked over her shoulder. "I should go," she mumbled. "Ugh. I wish this was a weekend. We could sit and chat for hours."

Jenna glanced at her watch. "I better get back. Hyacinth will be clock-watching."

"Thought you said she was a good boss?" Leigh queried.

"Those weren't my exact words." Jenna put the remainder of

her quiche into a napkin, and gulped down her glass of water. "I'll have to run back," she moaned.

"I should get going, too," said Merry. She would need to drive back to work and that would eat into her lunchtime. But she was desperate to know. "What are you two hiding from me?"

Jenna rolled her eyes. "You're not going to give it up, are you?"

No, she wasn't. Because it hurt for her to think that Dylan might be having second thoughts. "I'm stressed enough about the dress."

Leigh glanced at Jenna, then at Merry. "You're impossible to distract."

"Then don't distract me. Tell me," she begged, feeling a knot deep in her stomach.

"Your bachelorette party."

"What?" These were the last words she'd expected to hear.

"Jenna and I have been trying to organize it," explained Leigh.

Merry's mouth fell open. For a fleeting micro-second, she wasn't sure whether to believe them or not.

Jenna nodded in agreement. "We weren't sure if you wanted to go for a few beauty treatments. They have a boutique in Whisper Falls."

Merry's heart sank, even though the weight of Dylan's supposed doubt had been lifted. "Oh, girls," she said, trying not to gush. "You were really planning my bachelorette party?"

"You're getting married, aren't you?" Jenna shot back.

"That's really sweet of you. That would have been lovely."

"What do you mean that would have been? We'll do it, even if you move the wedding to later."

She looked at them both, believing them. She'd jumped so fast to the wrong conclusion that Dylan was having doubts, when she was the one who was thinking about postponing.

"We'll catch up over the weekend," said Jenna, kissing her on the cheek. "Don't worry. It's still Dylan you're going to end up marrying. Doesn't matter if it's a few months later or now. That man would wait forever for you." She rushed off.

"Let me know what you decide," said Leigh, staring at the uneaten slices of quiche on Merry's plate. "You didn't eat."

"I wasn't hungry."

Her friend packaged up the untouched food. "I'll hold off on the cake, if you decide to postpone."

"I'll let you know. Thanks for meeting me at such short notice."

"Hey, don't worry." Leigh handed her the food package. "You need to eat."

"I'm too stressed."

"You shouldn't be. Everything will work out. It always does."

CHAPTER 14

"How was your mom this morning?" Dylan asked Chloe, who was doing her homework at the kitchen table. She looked up, her hand paused as she stopped coloring the map she was working on. "She was like she is every day."

Dylan nodded, more to himself than anything else. He'd called Merry at work today to tell her that he would pick Chloe up from school, because he finished early at the store and Laura was happy to stay late, but the truth was, he didn't want Merry to fix dinner when she got back from work. He had noticed that she had been stressed out a lot these past few days, and he chalked it up to her being busy in her job at the department store. With Christmas approaching, she had started to do longer hours, and because she only worked three days, it seemed that she tried to finish everything in those three days.

On top of that, she had the advertising for the store to take care of. Despite her saying she could handle it, he could see that she was starting to struggle.

He didn't want her to struggle. It was bad enough him being stressed about the kiln, but they both couldn't be like that.

As for himself, he'd needed to step away from the gift store today and do something else to take his mind off the troubles which seemed to be springing up left, right and center.

The guy who had come earlier today to take a look at his kiln informed him that he needed a new part, and even thought he would order the part immediately, the part was out of stock and wouldn't arrive until early next week.

It left a month to his wedding. He wanted to stop working at least a few days, if not a whole week, before his wedding day, but at this rate, if he was to fulfil the vase order, he need to work flat out right up until the wedding.

The home furnishings store had placed an order for vases for December, and it was as big as the November order.

He was swamped, but he didn't want to call the manager and tell him that he would have difficulty in meeting the November order and that he couldn't even begin to think about the December order.

This kiln nightmare had mushroomed into a production problem which messed up his orders, his wedding, his mood. Thank goodness for the wedding. It seemed to be the only bright beacon of something good on the horizon.

When the guy had left, Dylan had called Merry to tell her that he'd be making dinner and that he would pick Chloe up from school.

It was probably just as well that he did because Merry sounded stressed out herself. She couldn't talk much, and she thanked him, then told him she would work a little later than usual, if it was fine by him.

Of course it was fine by him.

He didn't mind being the house husband tonight.

He liked spending time with Chloe, and he liked making life easier for Merry. Besides, who said only women did the cooking? He'd been handling things just fine, before Merry came along.

One day, maybe in the not so distant future, she would be

busy with a new baby, and he vowed to be a fully hands-on dad.

"Why?" Chloe asked, fiddling around with the felt-tip pen in her hand.

"Why what?" He'd lost his train of thought.

"Why do you want to know how mom was?"

"No reason." And then, because he knew kids were super smart and picked up on these things, he added, "I wanted to check if her fingers were still hurting."

Chloe shrugged. "I don't think so. She managed to put on her lipstick."

"Oh, good."

"Is that why you're making dinner?"

"That's right."

Chloe got back to her coloring, and he got back to fixing the dinner.

Merry got in from work two hours later than usual. He had almost given up waiting because he was starving.

She came in, saw the food, kissed him and thanked him, then rushed off to see Chloe. Her daughter was too old now for Merry to put to bed, but she still liked to catch her quickly, and briefly, to find out how her day had been. He waited for her and Chloe to have some alone time.

"At least you're had your dinner, buddy," he said to Spart, who sat on the floor, paws out, like a Sphinx. Dylan patted his own belly. "I, on the other hand, am starving." He nodded while Spart stared at him. "Starving, I tell you," he said, then felt foolish when Merry walked in and caught him talking to the dog.

"Did I interrupt something?" she asked, walking towards the kitchen.

"Man talk," said Dylan with a grin. He got up and followed her into the kitchen. "Sit down, I'll get your dinner."

"I can manage."

She looked stressed. Unsmiling. Tightly wound up. This

wasn't the effect he'd been hoping for. "I'll plate up for both of us."

She listened and sat at the table, while he made small talk, asked her about her day, and her staying late. She wasn't her usual self, and he was determined to get to the root of it all.

"Meetings," she said, when he sat down next to her. "A whole day spent on meetings."

He wasn't sure a day of meetings was entirely responsible for her mood, but instead of pressing her for information, he decided to wait it out. She would tell him in her own time.

They ate quietly. If she didn't open up soon, he would ask before he left to go back to his place. There was no way he could leave her like this. At times like this, he wished that they were already married and that he didn't have to leave and go home alone.

"What happened about your kiln?" she asked, as if suddenly remembering the guy was coming to look at it today.

He told her the sorry outcome.

"Next week?" She looked shocked. "But that will affect the number of vases you can make."

"I know. Once it's fixed, I'm going to have to work all night for as long as it takes in order to meet that commitment. And it gets worse..."

"Worse?" She looked alarmed. A little *too* alarmed, now that he saw the look on her face.

"The manager at the home furnishings store placed an even larger order for December."

Her eyes grew round. "But we're getting married soon."

"The kiln will be fixed by then."

"But you'll be working crazy hours to meet the December order, and you're already struggling with the November order."

"Don't worry, Merry. One way or another, I'll get it done, and if I can't, well, then I can't. What's the worst that can happen?"

But she looked worried. She always worried, and he didn't see the point in worrying about the smaller things in life. The orders, the kiln, these were the smaller things.

In the bigger scheme of things, getting married to Merry, thinking about a family home for them to live in—something they hadn't yet discussed—these were the bigger things.

Life things. And these mattered more. "What is it, Merry?" he asked, putting down his fork.

She looked at him rather pensively, he thought. It made him wary. "What is it?" he asked again, his voice softer.

"Maybe we should postpone?"

"Postpone what?" He had an inkling, but he needed clarification in case he got the wrong end of the stick.

"Our wedding."

He stopped eating and sat back. "You want to postpone our wedding?" That's what he'd been afraid she'd said. Now she had him worried. "Are you getting cold feet?" This had been his fear all along, that as time went on, she would get jittery.

December, and all that it meant for her, was full of bad memories; a wound too deep to ever fully recover from. This wasn't the end to the day he had been waiting for. Bad news about the kiln had hit him like a punch to his gut. He'd come over early today to be with the woman he loved. She made everything feel better, and he'd come here seeking solace even though he had sensed—after hearing her voice on the phone—that she, too, was feeling low.

But he hadn't expected *this* news.

She sighed a little too heavily, making his nerves frazzle. "I'm not getting cold feet," she said slowly.

"Then what is it?"

"What isn't it?" she mumbled, but he heard it, and it worried him. "You know I told you about the wedding dress I saw in Whisper Falls?" He nodded. "It's not for sale."

"Not for sale?"

"The owner called me a few days ago to apologize."

"A few days ago, and you're only telling me now?" This alarmed him, that she had hidden this news from him for a few days.

"You were worried about the kiln. I didn't want to stress you out even more."

"But you're stressed and worried, Merry, and I can't believe that you kept this to yourself."

She shrugged. "We've both had a lot of stuff to deal with."

"Tell me about the dress."

"It shouldn't have been out on the rack on display. Someone bought it the day before, but due to a series of errors—new staff and the shop owner not being around—it wasn't put away. So she called me first thing on Monday morning to tell me. It had already been sold, and they can't get me another one because the shop only sells one piece of a kind."

He blinked back his surprise, and tried to make sense of what she had told him. It didn't make sense. "You want to postpone our wedding because of the dress?"

She shrugged. "It's not just the dress. *Everything's* going wrong."

These were minor obstacles, and they could be overcome. It wasn't the end of the world. That would be if Merry decided she couldn't go through with the wedding. "The dress you liked isn't available. We can find another one. There are other shops, Merry, and we can look online."

"I had my heart set on that dress."

"You'll find something better."

"We don't have long, and we have so many other things to sort out. Finding Chloe something to wear that she and I agree on will take an entire weekend."

"It won't. She's so excited about the wedding, she'd wear anything you put her in."

Merry looked at him stunned. He stood by his words. Seemed to him that he had a different relationship with Chloe than Merry did. He found her easygoing, where there was more of a clash of horns sometimes between mother and daughter.

He refused to give in so easily, and he refused to let Merry sink into a pit of misery and feel down. "You've only been shopping this weekend, and you found the so-far-perfect dress. I guarantee you'll find something even better." He reached for her hand and held it, rubbing his thumb over her palm gently.

"What about your kiln? You're going to have to work right up until the day before the wedding. And you're going to be so stressed."

"But I get to marry you," he said. "That's the best ending to all these silly little problems."

She slapped a hand to her face and pushed her chair away, pulling her hand away from his. "The card. I didn't switch the card." She shot up from her chair.

He didn't understand. "What does that mean?"

"It means the ads haven't run for days."

"Don't you check them every day?" he asked, then regretted his words.

"Are you blaming me?"

He stood up slowly, realizing her deep frustration only now. "No. That's not what I meant. I thought you checked them every day."

"It's been a crazy few days."

He stepped towards her, tried to put his arm around her waist, but she stepped away. "Don't you see? It's a sign."

"A sign?" He leaned closer, refusing to let her push him away.

"A sign that we're rushing things."

"Things we can overcome," he said gently, but firmly. Did all brides get these pre-wedding jitters? He tried to reassure himself that this was normal.

"I need to switch the cards," she said, starting to move away, but he grabbed her hand.

"It can wait."

"No, it can't, Dylan. The ads stopped running, which means your online orders will have dropped."

"I don't care. I didn't have any online orders until a few months ago. It's not the end of the world."

"That's not the attitude to have when running a business."

"I'm not concerned about the business. I'm concerned about us." He wanted to get to the bottom of this, needed her to see that whatever problems they were experiencing were par for the course. They definitely were not a sign from the universe that they shouldn't get married.

"What about the credit card fraud? The $3,000 we didn't spend?"

"What about it?" he shrugged. "The bank will reimburse us. It's not as if we have to pay for that out of our pocket."

He held her hand. "Meredith, this isn't a good enough reason for wanting to postpone. Unless…" he waited for her to look into his eyes. "Unless you're having second thoughts?"

She blinked in response.

Not hearing the answer he had hoped for, he told her, "I love you, Merry. I love you more each day, and I can't wait to make you my wife." She looked more lost than ever. He had believed she had been ready to move on, and had put the past firmly behind her, but maybe this time of year resurrected all the old ghosts. It wasn't her fault.

If she wasn't ready, she wasn't ready, and though he hated to say it, he had to give her an out. "If you need more time, if you want to delay the wedding, we can." It wasn't what he wanted, but if it was what she wanted, then so be it.

CHAPTER 15

*S*he woke crying. Seeing Brian's face did that to her.

Sitting up in bed, it took a few moments before she realized that she had been dreaming. This wasn't real. But why had she been crying? Had she known, in her dream, that she was dreaming? That Brian wasn't really here?

In her dream, he had kissed her before leaving to go to work. He told her they would go shopping to buy a real Christmas tree on the weekend. He said he wanted Chloe to pick the tree this time because she was old enough. He'd kissed her, and Merry had kissed him back. The moment he'd walked out of the door, she had burst out crying.

She hadn't dreamed of Brian for months, ever since she had moved to Starling Bay.

What did this mean?

She got out of bed and did everything on autopilot; showered, dressed, had breakfast with Chloe then dropped her at school. Then she set off to work at the gift store as usual, but as she got out of her car and walked towards Fraser's, she glanced at the astrology shop. That was what Dylan called it, but neither of them really knew what it was.

In a spur-of-the moment decision, Merry changed her course of direction and walked towards Ella Ray's Mystic & Magic Shop. She already knew that Dylan had left earlier to visit the manager of the home furnishings store. He wouldn't know.

After last night's discussion, and her suggestion to Dylan to postpone the wedding, she wasn't sure how they had left things. Dylan hadn't pressed the matter further, and she wasn't sure what they had decided.

Later that night, she had checked her advertising figures after Dylan had left and had seen that the online store sales had plummeted. It had left her even more demoralized.

She had tossed and turned in bed for hours, and then woken up crying having dreamt of Brian. Sneaking around behind Dylan's back was so out of character for her, but she felt somehow compelled to seek answers.

Removing her engagement ring, she slipped it into her purse. She hadn't even made an appointment, but with her heart beating as if she'd run a mile, she took a deep breath and stepped into the astrology shop, feeling guilty.

She prayed that Laura wasn't looking out of the store window to see her.

Once inside, the soothing smell of lavender filled the air. Books were neatly lined up on some bookshelves, and other display units had crystals and various gems and ornaments stacked on them.

She had expected it to be dark inside, not bright and well-lit. The woman at the counter looked up and smiled.

"I'm looking for the owner," said Merry.

"I am the owner. I'm Ella." She stepped out from behind the counter and walked towards Merry. She had expected Ella to be wearing something exotic, long flowing robes or a tie-dyed long flared skirt, but the woman before her was in dark leggings, with furry boots, and a long sweater. She was petite and pretty, and

Merry's attention was drawn to her perfectly shaped thick, dark brows.

"You're from Fraser's, aren't you?"

Merry nodded. "Yes. That's right," she said, speaking in a low voice, as if someone might hear her. She glanced over her shoulder towards the door, fearful that Dylan or Laura might walk in, even though Dylan had gone out of town. The three of them, Dylan, Laura and her talked about this place with amusement, even though Merry sometimes stood up for Ella, citing that it wasn't all 'nonsense' as Laura and Dylan made it out to be.

"Nice to meet you," said Ella.

"I'm Merry."

They shook hands. She had only seen her on a few occasions, going in and out of the shop but Merry had never spoken to her.

"I don't have an appointment," said Merry.

"I have a free slot, so you came at the right time."

"Oh."

"Would you like a reading?" the woman asked.

Now that she was here and had been asked that question, she wasn't sure. "What sort of reading?"

"I can do a tarot card reading, or draw up your birth chart. It's best if you give me your date of birth so that I can draw up your chart, and then you can come back another time so that I can go through it with you."

She didn't have time for that, and if she left it for another time, she feared she might back out. "Can we do something quick?" Merry asked.

"The tarot then. Follow me."

Ella led Merry into a room behind a curtain. A row of candles flickered along a shelf. "Please, take a seat."

Merry did as she was asked, settling into the comfy velvet chair. It was a small room with crystals and 'believe' and 'inspire' written on two framed wall pictures.

"I work next door a few days a week, and I would rather my boss didn't know I've come to see you," Merry explained, being vague and evasive.

"Then you don't need to say anything to him."

"I meant you…" Merry cleared her throat. "I hope you won't mention it."

Ella's lips curved into a thin smile. "I won't. Everything is confidential here. Set your mind at ease."

Merry felt anything but at ease.

Ella handed her the deck and asked her to shuffle. Nervously, she did, wondering what these cards might reveal.

Despite telling Dylan once that she believed in these things, now she wasn't so sure. Sitting across the table from a stranger who was about to delve deep into her mind and proclaim to be able to foretell her future made her wonder.

But she was desperate for answers, for guidance, and she needed to know what to do.

"Don't worry," said Ella, laying the cards down.

"I'm not worried," Merry lied.

But what if she had a card of death, if such a thing existed? What if something bad was going to happen? Would she want to know?

It was too late to back out now.

She shuffled the cards.

"I can't see your future, I can't read your thoughts either," said Ella, as if she had somehow picked up on Merry's discomfort. "And remember, you are always in control."

Merry didn't say anything out of fear of influencing Ella's reading. While she read her astrology horoscopes if she happened to see them in a magazine, she had never been interested in tarot cards, but now that she was here, she was curious. Knowledge was power, and to know what was going to happen was to be forearmed, wasn't it?

"I see sudden upheaval and disaster..." began Ella. Merry leaned forward, her heart in her throat. This definitely wasn't what she wanted to hear.

"Now? You see this happening now?" A hint of desperation laced her voice.

"In your past."

She breathed out and looked at Ella, not wanting to confirm or deny anything.

Ella continued, turning another card over. "You have experienced a lot of insecurity and loss of faith to the point where you've become discouraged and disillusioned with life."

That certainly wasn't true. She'd had a new lease of life with Dylan. Unless this woman was talking about her life before then. Merry remained quiet, not wanting to say anything which might hint at a clue.

"This was many years ago," Ella continued, running her perfectly manicured finger over the cards. "In your past. You have experienced sudden loss, shock and unbearable sadness."

Merry blanched at the too accurate description. She thought back to the time of Brian's death, and all that had followed. "Maybe," she said.

"It was a long time ago," said Ella, "but you're a fighter and a tough woman, at least..." Ella looked up at her. "That's the image you want to portray. Deep down, you're not really like that. You're soft and vulnerable, and you haven't allowed anyone to take care of you in recent years."

Merry had to begrudgingly accept that Ella might be right, but she wasn't about to admit to it.

"The Fool, aaah." A twinkle glistened in Ella's eye. "There is someone around you, someone who cares for you. But he's quite different than you."

The fool? Merry's gut tightened. That didn't sound too good. "What about him?"

"He believes that anything is possible. He doesn't worry."

She didn't like the idea of Dylan being a fool. "Is he a person in my life?"

"He represents something new in your life. A new beginning, the start of a new journey."

Now she was confused, but she remained silent.

"It could signify a new beginning, a rebirth, a new start, children even."

Her ears pricked up. "Children?"

Ella nodded. "In your future."

Children? Did that plural include Chloe or not? True to her word, she didn't ask.

"You're unsure about something. A decision, the way forward," Ella continued.

Merry sniffled and pressed her lips together, contemplating. That was vague. "Isn't everyone unsure about something at some point?"

Ella didn't answer her, even though Merry was sure she didn't miss the hint of sarcasm in her voice.

"Give yourself permission to open yourself."

Merry scoffed. That was vague. "You mean like a door?" she asked, feeling disenchanted with the reading. So far it had been nothing but mumbo-jumbo. Ella had told her nothing new, and everything she said had a dozen different ways of being interpreted.

"As in stop doubting yourself," said Ella. "You're holding back, thinking too much of the past when the door to your future is open."

"Huh."

"The two of cups." Ella nodded. "You have a soul connection with this person."

"Which person?" she asked, wanting to be difficult.

"The person who is your soulmate. He's in your life now, and you each bring out the best in one another."

Obviously Ella would have seen her and Dylan out walking the dog. Even though they didn't see her around much, and she hadn't ventured into the gift store, as far as Merry could remember, this sort of observation wasn't hard to make. It would be obvious to most that she and Dylan were together.

"But you're doubting your feelings. About going ahead. There is a proposal, or a wedding or engagement?"

Merry breathed in as she weighed up Ella's comment. That was a given when two people were dating. If she'd kept her engagement ring on, would Ella have mentioned the word 'wedding', and not 'proposal' or 'engagement?'

"You're on the same wavelength. This partnership, this man, it is meant to be. The two of you are supposed to be together. He is someone who is very much at ease with himself. He doesn't chase riches, nor does he covet material things. He's been hurt."

"Hurt?"

"In the past. A past love. She broke his heart."

She shrank back, finding it painful listening to this stranger telling her about Dylan's ex-girlfriend. The dancer he had been madly in love with. Dylan hadn't told her this, but Jenna had when Merry had pressed her for more details, seeing that she wasn't going to get them from Dylan. She had needed to know. He had known all about Brian, but she couldn't bring herself to ask him too much about his ex, and she had sensed that he had never really wanted to talk about it. Now, Ella was confirming as much.

"There was someone," Merry said, but couldn't bring herself to say anymore.

"The two of you are meant to be. You complement one another. The way you met," she raised her eyebrow, "neither of you were looking for love, but something brought you together."

Merry opened her mouth, trying to fathom how much of this was Ella looking at the cards, and how much of it was her saying things as she saw them. For the chances were high she had seen her and Dylan strolling around hand in hand.

"You heal him," said Ella.

Merry ran those words through her mind. She *healed* Dylan? If anything, it was the other way around. He had been a healing comfort to her. He was the first man she had dated, the first man she had allowed herself to get close to after the tragedy, and now she felt as if she had known him forever.

Still, it hadn't stopped her recent doubts from surfacing, and all the things going wrong, and the dream about Brian. She wanted reassurance, a cast-iron guarantee that this time around theirs would be a happy ever after, forever.

"But what if bad things have happened and continue to happen?" she asked, in spite of her resolution to rein in her words.

"Every obstacle you meet is meant to be there," said Ella. "You are being tested, to see how much you want this."

Merry frowned. "But the obstacles. Aren't they a way of making you doubt?"

"Are they?"

Merry blinked. Ella answering her question with a question left her none the wiser. Merry glanced at her watch. She had things to sort out, the advertising to fix. Sitting here listening to some gobbledygook wasn't going to help her.

"Thanks, but I need to get back."

"But we're still in the middle of your reading."

"I need to go. You've been very helpful." She didn't mean this, because she was as puzzled as ever, but she didn't want to hurt the woman's feelings. Merry stood up. "I'm sorry to have taken up your time. How much do I owe you?"

Ella got up. "We didn't finish the reading, and so therefore, I won't accept a payment."

"But it was my fault we didn't finish."

"It's fine. Really it is."

"Thank you." She followed Ella out of the room.

"Remember, you're always in control of your life," said Ella. "Life doesn't happen to you."

Merry shrugged. "I'll try to remember that. Thanks." She started to walk towards the door.

"Sometimes we're too jaded to see the truth of things, but it's the younger ones who can see how simple things really are."

She had no idea what to make of this, but she thanked the woman again and left.

CHAPTER 16

"You're postponing your wedding? But why?" Reed wanted to know.

Dylan didn't know what to tell them. He didn't want to mention Merry's part in the postponement. After Reed's engagement falling through with Olivia, it seemed that their group of friends were jinxed.

But he wasn't worried.

This wasn't a Reed-Olivia type of situation.

More to the point, Merry was nothing like Olivia.

And he and Merry weren't splitting up. They were delaying their wedding and sticking to their original date of 'sometime next year.'

As far as he was concerned, he didn't need a venue, caterers, or wedding vows to prove or seal his love for Merry, but he understood that it was a woman's prerogative to want the best of things, especially for her big day.

"Merry wants to wait. We've had a series of unfortunate events, and it's made her think that this is a sign that we're rushing things."

"A sign?" Rourke asked.

"What sort of sign?"

Dylan looked upwards. "From the heavens, or the universe, or something."

"I'm sorry," Reed said.

"We're delaying it," Dylan pointed out, "we're not *canceling* it."

"I get that, I know," his friend replied hastily.

"What series of unfortunate events?" Rourke wanted to know.

He told them.

"Three thousand dollars?" asked Reed, incredulous.

Dylan pinched the bridge of his nose. "I know. Online fraud is horrific."

"But you'll get it all back," Reed said.

"I know that, too. We're in the process of getting it all back, but these things take time."

He then explained about the wedding dress fiasco.

"That explains it," said Rourke, jumping in. "Women and their wedding dresses. If that gets messed up, the whole thing is..." He ominously made a gesture as if was slitting his throat.

Dylan shook his head. "Slightly overdramatic there, aren't you?"

Since their discussion a few days ago about postponing their wedding, Merry hadn't said anything further. He didn't want to rock the boat by saying anything about it either. A postponement wasn't what he wanted, and so he was happy to leave things as they were. He understood that Christmas was a busy time of year for most people, and if there was to be no wedding, they would have to let their guests know as soon as possible, as well as cancel the venues and the catering.

For now, though, he was prepared to let things lie for a while and cancel at the eleventh hour only if he had to.

He knew Merry. Knew she panicked and worried, and often for reasons which soon smoothed over.

"Does this mean the bachelor party's canceled?" Rourke asked Reed.

This was news to him. "What bachelor party?" He wasn't a partying type, but the way he felt right now, he was in no mood to entertain the idea at all.

Reed stayed silent.

"Guys, thanks for whatever you were both planning, but no bachelor party, please."

"There's not going to be one now. Not if you're not getting married until next year."

"When next year?" Reed asked.

"Who knows?" He wasn't sure himself. He was content to give Merry time, to not have it be now, but he was dreading the idea that she might have cold feet the next time around. He didn't want to think about that until he had to.

"You've canceled the venue and the catering?" Reed asked. He was the one who had gotten Dylan a good rate on one of the banquet suites at The Grand Hotel.

"I'll cancel it. But I want to leave it for a week or so."

"You think you can get Merry to change her mind?" Rourke asked.

"No. I'm hoping she'll realize that herself."

"I told you so." This was her mother's reply when Merry told her that they were moving the wedding date to next year. "This is a bad time of year for you, Meredith."

It so wasn't the thing she wanted to hear.

"Thanks, Mom." After her visit to Ella yesterday, she was even more confused.

"But it is, Meredith. You're doing the right thing. I was worried that you were rushing into things too fast."

Merry rested her forehead on the palm of her hand while keeping her ear to the phone.

Dylan was out with his friends, and Chloe was watching TV. She wanted to tell her parents, even though she and Dylan hadn't discussed the wedding since her announcement to move the date back.

She wasn't even sure if he'd told his parents.

What she did know was that it was only fair to start letting people know as soon as possible.

Tomorrow, she would tell Jenna and Leigh that it was definitely canceled, because every day Jenna sent her messages or links to yet another wedding dress.

She was sick of seeing wedding dresses.

She hadn't even told her mother about the problems they had experienced, knowing that it would only set her mother off again with her 'I-told-you-so' on repeat like a stuck record.

She didn't want to give her mother more ammunition and tell her about all the things that had gone wrong, so she didn't mention any of them.

Nothing about the dress, or the credit card fraud, or the Dylan's kiln acting up.

Her mother loved Dylan and believed he was a wonderful man, but once she had an idea in her head and was convinced that the month of December was bad for Merry, there was nothing that would make her budge from the idea.

Merry was starting to wonder if she was second-guessing herself, or if this was life trying to tell her that this was not a good idea.

Confusion rained down on her from all sides. Even the visit to Ella had proved useless.

Maybe things would be clearer once she told her friends. Jenna and Leigh were good like that. They grounded her and made her see sense.

Jenna had been all for going shopping for wedding dresses, but Merry had persuaded her that she wasn't in the mood to wander around wedding shops, and certainly not to Whisper Falls of all places.

But her friends had insisted that they all meet up again. She sensed they wanted to cheer her up, and given that things were slightly awkward between her and Dylan at the moment, she was happy enough to look on the internet and shop from the comfort of her friend's home.

CHAPTER 17

*D*ylan was washing the breakfast dishes when Chloe asked the question.

"When are we going to go shopping for my dress?" she asked her mom. Merry looked up from her laptop. Then she looked at her daughter and then at him.

She hadn't told Chloe that the wedding was off, and he waited now with bated breath to hear what she would say.

"What?" asked Chloe, sensing that something was wrong given by the silence from both of them.

The girl looked at him, and he looked away guiltily. He would have told her, but he didn't feel this type of announcement should come from him.

"Mom?" Chloe marched up to the table where Merry sat with her laptop. It wasn't often that she brought the laptop to the kitchen table, but he could tell she was worried and distant too, and perhaps she was hiding behind the laptop and her excuse of having too much to do.

Things weren't cold between them but they also weren't the same as usual; fun, and easy, and peppered with kisses and cuddles. Something had changed between them over the past week or so, and neither of them seemed to want to broach the subject.

He had been determined to wait it out and see if Merry might change her mind about wanting to postpone the wedding. He'd been hoping that she might feel better as time went on, but instead she seemed to be even more aloof and distant with him.

He couldn't understand it.

"Honey, we're thinking of moving the wedding day to next year—"

"What?" Chloe looked at him, then at her mom, then at him again, as if he had the answer.

Dylan took a slow breath in. She'd gone and said it now. She'd told Chloe, which meant it was cast in stone. There was no going back. The decision had been made.

"We're not *not* getting married," Merry began.

He felt compelled to explain, to set the poor girl's mind at rest. "We've only postponed it until next year, Chloe."

"But why?" the girl cried. He looked at Merry for the answer, and she seemed at a loss as to what to say.

Not wanting to leave Chloe feeling upset, he said, "Your mom feels we might be rushing things, and she's right. Maybe we are."

"But you don't think that," Chloe threw back. "You said you'd marry my mom right away. That's what you said." Chloe spun around, "It's all your fault," she cried, her voice so venomous that it shocked him. He stopped washing the dishes and was about to go to her.

"Honey." Merry closed the laptop and pushed it away. "That's right. It wasn't Dylan's decision. It was mine."

"But why, Mom?"

Merry fidgeted with the ring on her finger and seemed to struggle to say something.

"You said Dylan made you really happy," Chloe challenged. "You look happy, you sound happy."

"I *am* happy." Merry fixed her gaze on him. "Dylan makes me feel all of those things, but," she sighed, "I don't have my dress, and things haven't gone right for us lately."

"So that's it? You've given up because you don't have a dress?" snapped Chloe, sounding years older than thirteen.

"No, I haven't given up, young lady." Merry replied crossly. She stood up and picked up her laptop. "What's the matter with you?"

Sensing that Merry was stuck and angry, and seeing that Chloe looked as if she was about to cry, Dylan waded in. "It's only a matter of a few weeks or months, Chloe." He looked to Merry for confirmation, found none, and looked away. "December is busy. The store is so busy. My kiln broke down, and it won't be fixed for a few more days. It's going to be an absolute nightmare for me. I can't marry your mom when I'm so overworked and tired. Your mom just wanted us all to be relaxed and take things easy."

"But if you let these things stop you now..." Chloe lifted her hands up in an all-is-lost gesture. He admired her tenacity. Chloe wasn't talking like a teen, but like a wise, older person.

And she was right.

He had to take Merry's side, even though he didn't agree with it. "I think there's no harm in waiting a while, Chloe."

"You're both always telling me never to give up and to do my best, and I can't see that you're doing that."

She stomped out of the kitchen with Spart following her.

Dylan wiped his hands dry and looked at Merry.

"She hates me," said Merry.

"She doesn't hate you. She's just angry."

"Are you angry?" Merry asked him.

"At you? No. I could never be angry at you."

She opened her mouth as if she was going to say something, but seemed to change her mind.

"I told my parents," she said.

He nodded. "I told my friends."

"What did they say?"

"They were surprised. They'd planned the bachelor party."

She smiled, and these days even that was a rare thing. "That's what Jenna and Leigh told me. I told them I wasn't in the mood for partying."

"That's what I said," said Dylan. Everything about him and her being together pointed to them being a good team. A great couple. Two people who understood each other, thought alike and had the same views.

"Jenna insists we look at more wedding dresses."

His heart skipped a beat.

"But I don't see the point in looking right now."

In an instant, his hopes sank like the Titanic.

"Then let's do something," he suggested. "Let's go out for the day." All of a sudden he wanted to do something fun, something spontaneous as a family. Anything to take their mind off this cloud of despair that seemed to hang over them.

Merry made a face, and he knew his idea was as good as dead. "I told Jenna I'd go over to her place. Leigh's coming too. We're going to look online for dresses."

He couldn't be annoyed about that.

"I'll take Chloe out, see if I can cheer her up," he offered.

"I didn't think she would be that upset."

He did. The girl wanted them to be a family, as he did. It surprised him that Merry couldn't see that.

CHAPTER 18

With Chloe's outburst so fresh in her mind, Merry had even less interest in looking for wedding dresses online. It also didn't help that things between her and Dylan had cooled even more.

He was being supportive, and he hadn't said anything, hadn't been in a sour mood or off with her, but that was the problem. He hadn't said anything about the wedding. He had been particularly helpful when Chloe had exploded in anger at the news, but she felt almost as if he agreed with Chloe. It left her feeling guilty.

The small things were easy, dinner and the store, and Chloe and Spart, but the bigger things they avoided talking about. She didn't like it and knowing Dylan, he probably didn't either, but they were stuck in an impasse and neither of them seemed to know how to move beyond it.

Going to Jenna's place was a welcome relief, and when Leigh showed up soon after, the three of them wasted no time, at Jenna's command, in looking online for wedding dresses. Jenna had put a list together of reputable online stores, and they slowly worked their way down it.

But Merry's heart wasn't in it.

Even when she had told them that the wedding was definitely off, they seemed to think it would happen a few months later in the new year.

"Can't we just sit around and talk?" she asked, climbing off the kitchen stool and walking over to admire the lilies in Jenna's glass vase.

Fresh flowers cheered up a room more than any painting, in her opinion. She touched the soft petals, and let her fingers trace around the cold glass.

"We're only looking," said Jenna.

"What is it?" Leigh asked.

She told them about Chloe's outburst.

"She's upset," said Leigh.

"I don't blame her," added Jenna. "Poor kid. She was probably getting excited that her mom was going to get married."

Merry understood that. Chloe was fond of Dylan, and he doted on her. In that way, Merry knew that she was lucky to have met a man like him. Not all stepfathers were that good.

It had been one of the things that had put her off dating, the idea that she would have to let someone else in, when so far it had been just Chloe and her. With Dylan, that problem had never surfaced. He'd slowly slipped into and become a part of their lives without her feeling she was giving some of her love for Chloe to someone else. Dylan gave, and he adored Chloe. The fact that she had never had to worry about him or Chloe getting along spoke volumes.

Jenna jumped off her stool. "She sees how happy you are with him, Merry. You tell me what child doesn't want that?"

Merry folded her arms, feeling defensive. Ella's words still floated around in her head, mixing with Chloe's angry words, leaving her feeling worn out.

"I'm not in the mood to shop for wedding dresses."

"That's okay," said Leigh. "We just thought you might want to find the perfect wedding dress now, while your mind was still fresh with the images of the other one."

"Don't talk to me about the other one."

She caught Jenna and Leigh looking at each other again.

"What?" she asked, knowing that her surliness was out of character. She wasn't one to get hung up over a dress, or to make a scene and get all moody, but today she was so not in the mood for anything.

"If you don't want to look for it yet, we don't have to," said Leigh.

"What are you scared of, honey?" Jenna asked.

She paused a moment before answering. Something Jenna had said struck a chord. Maybe it was fear that made her doubt her decisions, fear for the unknown future, that made her second guess.

The visit to Ella's shop hadn't helped. Thoughts about Brian and the past had resurfaced, colliding with her desires for her future with Dylan. The past and present mingled and collided, leaving her battered, bruised and teary.

One chapter of her life was ending, and a new one was beginning.

It didn't matter what anyone said, change was scary. Even getting married to a man she was madly in love with was scary.

Her friends had the gift of not knowing, of not being blindsided by tragedy. They naively believed that 'I do' led to happy ever after.

It wasn't Dylan she had doubts about, it was the fear of losing her happiness all over again.

It was the fear of stepping into this shiny new happy world with the full knowledge that it could all be ripped from her at any time.

This was what life had taught her.

And Dylan understood her, because this man, whom she loved with all her heart and soul, knew her fears at some deep, unspoken level.

Her saying 'I do' was scary because it was a blank slate, a brand new page of a whole new chapter in an empty book. It was waiting to be written, and the ending was uncertain, a happy ending not guaranteed.

"Merry?" asked Jenna, gently touching her arm. "What are you scared of, honey?"

"That I could lose it all over again," she murmured softly.

Her friends rushed to her side; Leigh rubbing her arm, and Jenna putting her arm around her shoulder.

"That's a chance we all have to take," said Leigh. "I haven't experienced a loss like yours, and I hope I never do, but I had my own version of hell with Hank before I met Rourke."

Jenna squeezed Merry's shoulder. "And you know, I positively hated Reed before we started dating."

Merry chuckled, knowing the full story of Jenna and Reed's romance.

"You worry too much," Leigh told her.

She knew that. "That's what Dylan says."

"We can't predict our endings," Leigh continued, "but we can do our best to shape them how we want, even though life sometimes has other plans."

"Life *always* has other plans, but it doesn't mean you have to live and cower in fear," said Jenna. "If I'd done that, I'd still be a broke waitress living on noodles instead of ending up with Reed Knight. I would never have taken a chance and shown up on his doorstep, willing to be his maid."

It was fear that had paralyzed her. Fear that seeded doubts in her head. Fear that made her see everything as a reason not to go forward with her plans. She already felt so much better for listening to her friends. "Thanks, girls. I don't know what I'd do without you."

"Oh, you'd be fine," said Jenna. "You're not one to fall to pieces."

Then why had she had a mini crisis of sorts now?

"We're not telling you to get married as soon as possible."

"No, we're not." Leigh told her.

"We're just telling you that you have to stop being so scared."

"Is that what you think this is?" Merry asked them as something dawned on her.

"I'm not a psychic," said Jenna, grinning, "but yeah, that's what I'm saying."

"What *we're* saying," said Leigh.

The psychic reference was uncanny, and there was no way her friends could have known that she had visited Ella.

Jenna grinned at her. "There's nothing wrong with a wedding next year. It will be something to look forward to."

Maybe preparing for the wedding had shaken her core. This wasn't about getting the perfect wedding dress, it was about having something and losing it. Like she had Brian. The dress reminded her that she was about to take that chance all over again with someone new, and even though she felt blissfully happy, deep down she still had fears of stepping into a new unknown.

Postponing the wedding was the best thing to do. "This year is almost over, and it's so busy already. A spring wedding will be easier."

She was thinking of Dylan. As soon as the kiln was fixed, he was going to start on the vase order for November. He only had a week to go to get them all done, and Thanksgiving was already upon them.

At least their families weren't coming to visit and were still sticking to their original plans of coming at Christmas.

Family, she thought, feeling slightly elevated at the thought of meeting Dylan's parents. She needed more time to get to know them, and for them to get to know her and Chloe. A spring wedding definitely made more sense.

CHAPTER 19

When she returned after seeing her friends, Merry seemed less stressed out. Happier. Wearing the smile he had come to love. It gave him hope, even though things were still slightly frosty between Chloe and her mom. Dylan resolved to have a word with Chloe tomorrow while Merry was away.

He didn't ask her anything outright. All he'd known was that Merry and her friends were still looking at wedding dresses in a bid to find one that she loved as much as the one she had fallen in love with.

He hoped that her relaxed expression was an indication of good things, and it was only later, when they were curled up on the couch watching TV, that she threw the bombshell at him.

"I told Leigh to hold off on the cake."

The words landed like a punch to his stomach. He turned to face her. "You did?"

She looked at him doe-eyed. "I know we haven't really discussed it…"

"We haven't."

She bit her lip, a soft sigh escaping from her mouth. "I feel like I'm making the decision, and you're agreeing with me."

"As opposed to what, Merry?" He reached for her hand. "You said we're rushing into it and there's no need. You're not wrong, but I'd still marry you tomorrow if I could."

"Chloe hates me. She doesn't understand."

"She will. She was just getting excited. Another month won't make much difference."

She bit her lip again, and he waited for the second bombshell. "A spring wedding sounds nicer, don't you think?"

"Spring?" In his head he'd prepared himself for a wedding early in the new year. Sometime in January had been his thinking.

Not spring.

"It's a nicer season, and the weather is better," she continued. "You won't have the pressure of all those vases hanging over your head."

She was trying to justify it. It didn't matter if he had a thousand vases to make, he would have made them. He would have done what needed to be done in order to clear up his time for the wedding.

Christmas or no Christmas.

"You don't like the idea of a spring wedding?" she asked. He knew she was nervous, despite her confident announcement. He rubbed her hand gently with his thumb.

"I want whatever you decide is best. Whenever you're ready."

That was the question. Would she be ready in spring? Getting married was a big step for each of them, but in some ways it was easier for him to take than it was for her. He understood, which was why he wanted to give her a wide berth.

"Don't worry about it. So, what did you and the girls do?" They obviously hadn't been talking about wedding preparations.

"Jenna had a list of wedding dress stores online. We started to go through those." Merry rested her head back on the sofa and looked up. "I don't know why she's so obsessed about finding me the perfect wedding dress."

"I guess it's because she wants you to find something you loved as much as the other one."

"Is that what you think?" Merry asked him.

"That's what Reed mentioned. You think we guys don't talk?"

"What do they think, Reed and Rourke, of us postponing it?"

He hadn't confirmed it for definite the last time, but he could see that he would have to tell everyone now so that they could all cancel their arrangements. "They're guys. They don't think of it in any great detail."

She rested her head on his shoulder. "I'm sorry."

"Hey," he lifted her head up gently, then twisted his body around so that he could face her. "What are you sorry about? It's a few months later, that's all."

"I'm the one who rushed to get married in December," she reminded him. He had been the one to caution her about it, and as things had turned out, he had been right.

"I guess I'll be busy making vases for the next few weeks." There was no need to rush the order through and work all through the nights once his kiln was fixed.

"You can go easy on the December order. You can spread them out now and make some every week since we won't be going anywhere."

No wedding, and no honeymoon.

It would free up his time. "But we have family coming to stay over Christmas," he told her.

"Although they won't need to stay for as long."

Even so, it would still mean interruptions in his schedule. "I haven't even told my parents."

Merry gasped. "You haven't?"

He shook his head. He'd been holding out on telling people, hoping that Merry would change her mind. He was going to have to tell Laura that she didn't need to cover the store over the holidays, since they were no longer going away.

"We need to tell everyone we invited," he said. "And Blake and Shay. I'd invited them to the pre-wedding dinner as well." He had gotten to know Blake through Reed, and he liked the guy. And Shay was Jenna's good friend, so they had often run into one another and become good friends.

"Jenna said they were seeing each other. She was shocked!"

"Shocked?"

"She said she'd never seen it coming," Merry told him.

"People meet in all sorts of ways. Look at us."

She smiled. "Look at us."

He moved forward and kissed her, but as he started to pull away, she put her arm around his neck and pressed her lips down harder, rewarding him with a full-blown kiss that set his insides on fire.

He groaned. This was why getting married sooner would have suited him. He hated leaving Merry and going back out into the cold in the dark of night to return home alone. He hated that they were living in two different places.

But everything in good time; he tried to remember this even when, at times like now, it was difficult. When Merry looked up at him and the warmth of her embrace made it almost impossible for him to drag himself away and leave.

"I should go. It's getting late."

"So soon?"

"The guy is coming early to fix the kiln, and I'm going to be working like a fiend."

She kissed him again, tempting him. "You're teasing me, Merry," he groaned, forcing himself to pull away.

"I've missed you."

"I've been here all along," he said, but he knew what she was hinting at. Not wanting to touch on wedding talk, they had skirted around that conversation, but making a firm decision now had somehow melted all the tension between them.

"I hate it when we don't talk freely."

He tucked a stray hair behind her ear. "We've had our first official disagreement, and it was about our wedding. That's saying something, don't you think?"

"My daughter hates me."

"I'll talk to her tomorrow. She's upset."

"I know she's upset," said Merry. "She told me that she was looking forward to us all waking up together on Christmas morning and opening the presents under the tree."

Even though he wasn't a father, he understood perfectly why Chloe was angry. Because of her father's accident, and because Merry had been so angry around Christmastime, things probably hadn't been all that great at home for her, no matter how hard Merry would have tried to hide her feelings from her daughter. He sensed in Chloe a longing for an alternative Christmas morning.

"She just needs to talk it out, her feelings are probably all over the place," he said. He would ask her why she was upset, and then he would listen, and then he would explain their decision to her. It wasn't anyone's fault, it was just the way things were.

"I love you," she told him, and it looked as if she was going to say something else. He cocked his head, waiting for a few seconds, but she stayed silent.

"I love you, but I'm going to have to leave you." He forced himself to standing, even though she didn't let go of his hand easily.

A spring wedding wasn't ideal, it wasn't what he wanted, but it was better than nothing.

CHAPTER 20

Thanksgiving came and went, and the store became busier. With the ads restarted on the online store, the sales were slowly starting to creep back up again. Merry felt a huge sense of relief.

Also, the bank had been in touch to reassure them that everything had been put to right with their business credit card. It was another piece of good news.

Merry stared each time she walked past Ella's store. Now that she had met the owner and had put a face to the mysterious woman they hardly ever saw, the place wasn't a complete mystery to her anymore. She had no further desire to return. Ordinarily, she was a levelheaded person most of the time, and she now looked back on that visit as a glitch. It had been panic that had compelled her to go looking for answers in the first place, and she had promptly dismissed everything Ella had told her.

She chalked it up to her situation, and maybe even the season, for it had been a year ago when the panic attacks and anxiety had set in. Back then, her boss had signed her off from work for a few months, and it was that very action that had led Merry to come to Starling Bay for much needed rest.

This time of year did that to her. Maybe it wasn't the fear of getting married that had made her doubt her decision, but the usual anxiety around this month.

Even so, it had been something she had wanted to change, but things hadn't worked out quite the way she had envisioned.

"Is Dylan still in the workshop?" Laura asked. "I haven't seen him all morning."

She had just arrived, and it was her first day of work at the store this week. "I expect he is." He'd been working around the clock ever since the kiln got fixed a few days ago.

"That man is going to kill himself," said Laura. "He's barely stopped to eat."

This was news to her. "Not even for lunch?"

"Not that I've seen. He doesn't want to let the home furnishings store down." There was nothing new in what Laura had said. It was a combination of factors which made Dylan strive to work harder, to do what it took, to meet the order. Whether it was because Reed had helped him get this deal, or because of the prestige and income he saw from the order, Dylan was a man of principles and a hard-working man who would never let anyone down.

"He's even more motivated because of the downtime with the kiln." The faulty kiln had only added to his stress.

Laura looked at Merry for a moment longer than usual. "I'm sorry to hear the news."

Merry frowned at the shop assistant. "What news?"

"Dylan told me that the wedding was off."

"Ahh, yes." She lowered her head and sighed. "We decided to postpone it."

"That's such a shame." The older woman continued rearranging the coffee cups on the display stand. Merry wasn't sure what to say to that.

"At least you won't have to work here during the Christmas break."

"I would have gladly worked here. That poor man was so looking forward to going on his honeymoon, getting away, just the two of you. I expect you both were looking forward to a break. That vase order and the kiln. It was just bad timing."

Merry didn't understand at first, and then it slowly dawned on her. Rather than blame her, Dylan had used the excuse of the vase order as the reason they had canceled the wedding.

"I expect you'll both be in need of a break by the time he catches up with everything."

Before Merry could answer, a customer came up to them and asked Laura a question. Merry took this chance to go and find Dylan.

But as she walked into the workshop, the sight of him slumped over the worktop sent her into shock.

No, not again.

She flew to his side, frantic with worry as she tried to rouse him. Her heart thundered somewhere in her throat.

She thought of the worst.

But in the next second, he lifted his head.

She allowed herself to breathe.

"Wh—what?" Dylan yawned, then scrubbed his face with his hand. It had been fleeting, but in that one tiny moment of dread, when she had thought the worst, a thousand regrets flew across her mind. "Thank goodness," she murmured and threw her arms around his neck, clinging to him tightly.

"Hey…" he hugged her back, and she slowly moved her head away and stared into his just-woken eyes. "Merry?" he said, as if he didn't understand what was going on. But he must have seen the frightened look in her eyes.

"What's wrong? What happened?" When she didn't answer,

because her throat muscles refused to work, he looked scared, and jumped up from his seat. "What's wrong? Is it Chloe?"

A sigh escaped her lips. It was silly, and real, and scary all at the same time.

"You were asleep," she whispered, as if it was the most painful thing she had ever seen. "You were only asleep."

He scrubbed a hand over his face. "Darn it. I only meant to put my head down for a quick forty winks and I must have slept right through."

"Right through the night?" she cried.

"I need to get these done."

"Dylan!" Now she was annoyed. "You can't pull all-nighters. They're not good for you."

He stretched out and yawned again. "I don't plan to make a habit out of it, Merry. I just wanted to get these done so that we could at least enjoy Christmas."

"How many nights have you done this?"

"A couple."

Her eyes widened. "Dylan!" she cried. "This isn't good for your health. You're going to make yourself sick."

"But I've got you to take care of me." He grinned at her, and she wanted to shake him hard and shake some sense into him. "I prefer to take care of you when you're in good health."

"I've caught up with November's orders."

She shook her head as she exhaled. At least that was something. Now that that was out of the way, he could take it easy.

"Hey," he yawned again, but this time, he pulled her towards him. "Good morning. Don't look so angry, Merry. I've had a lousy night, and your smile is the one thing that cheers me up."

She smiled.

"That's better." He reeled her in and hugged her.

"Will you please promise me not to sleep here through the night again?"

Instead of giving her the confirmation she wanted, he said, "I'm going home to shower and sleep for a while, and then I'll be back in the afternoon."

"What for?" she asked, worried for his health. "Now that you're all caught up with the vases, can't you take the day off today?"

He laughed, and looked at her as if she wasn't making sense. "I still have December's orders to do."

She let out a groan. "December's orders?"

"Larger than what I had for November."

This wasn't good. "Are they breaking your vases or selling them?"

He laughed. "Selling them, I'm sure, on account of the commission I'm getting."

She put her arm around his waist and nestled her head against his chest. "You work too hard."

"We had a glitch with the kiln, and it's messed up my production. This wasn't supposed to happen."

She looked at him but said nothing.

This wasn't supposed to happen.

Life and its curveballs. The things that weren't supposed to happen often did, and out of the blue. The things that were supposed to be plain sailing and were taken for granted, those things blindsided people when the worst happened. "I don't want you to make yourself sick," she told him.

"I won't, and now that the wedding's off, I have nothing else to do but carry on and finish these. I can, and we can have a great Christmas, have one like Chloe wanted."

"Chloe wanted you to stay over, so that we can open our presents together and spend the whole day together." Her daughter didn't ask her for much, and it had been needling her that the only thing she wanted—for her and Dylan to be married —was the one thing Merry couldn't give her.

"I can still stay over. I'll sleep on the couch, if it helps. If your parents are staying with you, and if they won't mind."

"They're staying at the hotel. They made their reservations for the wedding, and they've kept them. Stay over and we can give Chloe the type of Christmas she wants," Merry insisted.

"Next year," said Dylan, standing up and stretching. "Next year will be the year, right?" He said it like it was a question, as if he was asking her for real, if next year things would be all right.

"Of course. Next year, we'll be married." For sure, and maybe, if they both decided on it, she might be pregnant too. Next year would be different.

He kissed her on the lips and left the store.

She worked in Dylan's office for the rest of the day, and when he returned later in the afternoon, he still looked tired and disheveled, even though he'd claimed he'd slept.

As she got ready to go pick Chloe up from school, she tried to get Dylan to come with her. "Take the day off," she pleaded. He still looked so haggard and worn out.

"I can't, Merry. I have work to do."

"You can take a day off. You've earned it. You deserve it." She'd make a nice dinner, and maybe they could all sit in front of the TV and watch a nice Christmas Hallmark movie.

"I need to fulfill December's orders." He kissed her on the top of her head.

There was no stopping him. Even if they had gotten married this month, he would have insisted on finishing everything beforehand. The man was a workaholic.

"Come over for dinner later?" she asked.

"Don't I always?"

"Then stay to watch a movie with me and Chloe." She was overcome by a desire try to fulfill Chloe's wish as much as she could, and the idea of the three of them watching a cozy Christmas movie had popped into her head from nowhere. Now, she suddenly wanted it.

"I wish I could." He stroked her cheek. "But I don't like letting people down." He kissed her on the lips. "I'll be over for dinner, but I can't promise to stay for long."

At least that was something.

She grabbed her car keys and left, feeling a little sad and empty, and not knowing why.

CHAPTER 21

All talk of the wedding had been pushed to the side, and it was Christmas that everyone was looking forward to.

Dylan stared at the mirror and contemplated the reflection of the ragged-looking man who looked back at him.

Through a heroic shift of focus, and a few all-nighters which Merry continually told him off about, he was halfway through completing his vase order. While this was cause for some sort of victory, he knew he couldn't rest until the order was complete. He had been so focused on these that he hadn't had time to make more of the handmade products for which his store was known; the pet feeder bowls, and coffee mugs and Christmas tree ornaments, among other things.

Last night he had worked through to the morning, making sure he had enough of those. It was with immense relief that he now found himself looking forward to taking a break over the festive period.

It wasn't going to be the break he had longed for, but he welcomed the chance of sitting at home with family and doing nothing but eating and watching TV.

Of course, with both sets of parents over, it was going to be a busy time. He and Merry would be lucky to get to spend much time alone together, as well as with just the two of them and Chloe. Still, he hoped it would give his parents a chance to get to know Merry and Chloe.

He let out a loud sigh.

If only things had worked out. He would much rather have whisked Merry away. The idea of it being the two of them, and having no interruptions, appealed now more than ever because they had never had that kind of time alone to themselves.

Resigned to the way things were, he splashed cold water over his face and hoped that it would make him look more alive.

Tonight, he planned to work only until two in the morning. But first, he was going to Merry's place for dinner. Merry's place and his place. He was always going from one place to the next, and it left him feeling unsettled. Worse, he hated having to make a move once he had settled at her place, hated coming home to an empty house full of silence.

At least now he had a taste of the kind of life that would soon be his, and that in itself was a reason to be grateful.

She greeted him with a big smile, a huge hug, and a full-blown kiss—things which he loved and had come to take for granted. But, he'd noticed that she had been extra lovey-dovey and extra huggy ever since she had found him asleep in his workshop last week.

He took it as a sign of her concern. Clearly, she was worried about his health, and that he was going to drive himself to death with his crazy working hours.

As he walked into her living room, he saw the tree which the three of them had put up last weekend. That, and the aroma of something delicious cooking in the kitchen, grounded him. He suddenly didn't want to leave and go to work, even though he hadn't even had his dinner yet.

He walked over to the tree and stared at it while memories

from last year flooded back; he recalled the slow stop-start of his and Merry's relationship, the first time he met Spart and Chloe, and of Merry breaking down in the dark in the middle of a cold winter's night when he'd vowed not to come home until he found her.

A whole year had passed in the blink of an eye, and so many things in his own world had changed. His world was so much better.

"What are you doing?" Merry asked, sneaking up on him from behind and sliding her arms around his stomach. She pressed against his back, and he felt his heartrate quicken, felt the heat building in the base of his stomach. Regret and desire swept around him like a cool summer breeze. He wanted to pick her up and sweep her away, needed to love her, be with her and hold her, and it killed him that he had to wait before he could make that dream a reality.

"I'm admiring the tree," he replied, putting his hands over hers. She nestled her face in his back. "What are you doing?" he asked.

She hugged him tighter in response, but said nothing, and it confirmed that she was definitely more tactile, more loving and attentive of late.

They sat down and ate, and talked about the day each of them had had, taking turns back and forth. It was getting to be something they did every day. Later, when he offered to help them clear away the table, Merry and Chloe told him to sit down and relax a bit while they did it.

"How many more vases?" Chloe asked when they all sat down to watch TV. Merry sat snuggled up against him, and he put his arm around her shoulder, causing her to lay her head against his chest. He liked sitting with her like this. Loved the warmth of her body heat and the sweetness of her scent. Loved that she was his.

"Another thirty."

Chloe made a face, then her expression changed to one of confusion. "How many nights is that?"

"How many nights?"

Merry lifted her head. "She means how many all-nighters are you going to have to pull in order to get those done?"

He looked at Merry. "Did you put her up to this?" he asked, grinning.

"She's as concerned about your health as I am."

"Not many," he told Chloe.

"Mom says you're going to make yourself sick."

"I'm not going to make myself sick, I promise."

"You can't promise stuff like that," Chloe retorted.

He felt ganged up on with both mother and daughter worried about his health. And it felt good to have them be concerned—not that he wanted to cause anyone alarm—but it was a good feeling to know that they cared.

"I'm working hard now so that come Christmas day, we can do nothing but have fun."

"Mom says you're going to have a sleepover here," said Chloe. "Are you?"

He chuckled. "A sleepover?" He grinned at Merry. "I guess I am."

Chloe's grin was priceless.

Another Christmas movie started up on the television and he groaned, not wanting to leave, but not wanting to get too comfortable, either. If he stayed here for another half an hour, it would be impossible for him to get up and go to his workshop. "I'm going to go," he announced, and started to shift, but Merry didn't peel herself off him as he thought she would.

"Stay," she begged, not looking at him and not moving herself away from him.

"If I go now, I can be done by two in the morning."

"Stay for a bit," she pleaded.

Chloe must have heard because she piped up too. "Watch half of this new movie with us, *please*."

He looked at the Christmas tree all lit up, at Chloe sitting with a cushion on her lap, at Spart lying on the floor, and felt a warmth radiate through him. He hugged Merry closer to him.

He had no desire to get up and walk away from this, to go to his empty workshop and mold clay all night long.

"I'll watch half of it."

Merry reached for his hand and placed it in hers.

He had fallen asleep.

Merry carefully and gently extricated herself from his arm, and stood up.

"What about his vases?" Chloe whispered. "He said he needed to make them."

"They can wait." She walked over and picked up a thick blanket from the ottoman.

"Aren't you going to wake him, Mom?"

No, she was not. The poor man was shattered. She could tell from the moment he'd walked in. She wanted to marry him, not have him get sick and...

She draped the blanket over him and considered trying to get him to lie down in a horizontal position, but she didn't want to risk waking him.

"What are you going to do, Mom?" Chloe whispered. There was a hint of excitement in her voice which was hard to miss.

"I'm going to let him get his much-needed sleep. Off to bed for you, too, honey," said Merry, as her daughter refused to make a move.

"But won't he be angry with you? He said those vases were

important."

She disagreed. "His sleep is more important." She turned to face her daughter. "Bedtime, Chloe. Now."

Her daughter smiled. "I think it's cool he fell asleep. He feels like this is his home."

"Or he was tired," replied Merry.

"But he does like it here," Chloe insisted. "Think about it, Mom. He has no one at home. He doesn't even have a pet."

Merry folded her arms, waiting to see where her daughter was going with this. "I'm not kicking him out, Chloe."

Her daughter pressed her lips together, as if she was trying to stop herself from speaking. Merry wondered if she was still blaming her for postponing the wedding.

As things stood, Merry had started to blame herself for that, too. Lately, she'd started to wonder how things would have been had she stuck to her original plan to get married a few days before Christmas. A feeling of regret had started to seep under her skin, especially with the way things were going with Dylan almost killing himself by working so hard.

He said he didn't like to let people down, but she had been the one who had let him down.

Chloe rushed away without saying a word, causing Merry to frown, but in the next moment, her daughter returned with a pillow.

"Thanks, honey. I'm sure he'd appreciate that," Merry whispered. She put the pillow on the end of the couch. Dylan's body was leaning towards that end of the couch, where Merry had been propping him up. It wouldn't be long before he was completely horizontal, and, she hoped, that he'd lie down without waking up.

"Come on. Time to get to bed. All of us," she said, glaring at Spartacus. He seemed to understand, since he dutifully trotted off towards his dog bed.

CHAPTER 22

He woke up and gasped when he looked at his wristwatch.

It was half past eight.

He bolted upright and saw Spartacus looking up at him with his big brown eyes.

"You should have woken me up, buddy." Dylan stood up and couldn't believe that he had slept right through the night.

And Merry had let him sleep right through it.

He looked around for the keys to his pickup, and at the same time wondered where Merry was.

He didn't have to wonder for long.

"How are you feeling, Sleepyhead?" She leaned against the doorway, in her bright red Christmas sweater.

"You didn't wake me," he said, still looking around for his keys.

"You were tired. Zonked out completely."

"I have vases to make, Merry."

She walked towards him with her hands in her back pockets. Looking a little brazen, he thought, for someone who should have looked a little guilty on account of letting him sleep.

"So go and make them. You should be fully reinvigorated now that you've had the sleep you sorely needed. But first, breakfast." She stopped directly in front of him, preventing him from taking another step. And heck, not only did she look good in red, but she smelled good. He was always a sucker for her scent.

"I can't…I can't have breakfast," he said, trying to be firm. "I don't have time." He could have made a dozen vases by now and fired them in the kiln.

"Sweetie," Merry stood in his way, preventing him from going into the kitchen where he was certain he'd left his keys. "You can't leave without having breakfast," she insisted.

"Honey, you don't understand. Have you seen my keys anywhere?" He glanced around the room again.

"I've got them."

He looked up, blinked at her calm expression. "*You've* got them?" He scoffed. "I've been looking all over here for them. What are you doing with them?"

"You'll get them back once you've had a good breakfast."

He opened his mouth to protest.

"You've been working hard and you're tired, and I love you and I want to make sure you're taken care of. This is me taking care of you."

He tried to smile. This was all well and good, but did she have any idea of how much time his falling asleep had already cost him? "I want to finish up the vases before Christmas. The store needs them."

"Any chance you can get them done even earlier?"

He was about to answer when he realized he didn't understand her question. "Earlier?" He was sure he had misheard. She nodded.

"Why?"

"So that we can get married on the twenty-third, like we initially decided."

He jerked his head back, appraised her carefully, looking for signs of this being a huge, sick joke. "Don't kid me, Merry. It's not funny."

"It's not supposed to be funny. I'm being serious."

He couldn't believe his ears. "You...you... are you being serious?" He tried to think what had brought this on, tried to gauge if this was another rash decision she might go back on.

She nodded. "Completely serious."

"Why? What's brought this on?" He was still cautious. Still didn't know whether to believe her or not. This was a complete turnaround. His spirits had started to lift, but he was too afraid of getting excited and then crashing to the ground in dismay.

Merry pressed her hand against her chest and paused before answering. She looked calm and peaceful, something he had noticed about her since yesterday. It seemed that she had stopped worrying. "I panicked, I got scared. I let my doubts get the better of me."

"Doubts about what? Us?"

"About me, about being scared to go through this commitment again."

He cupped her face. "The way you say it makes it sound as if it's a heavy weight to carry."

She shook her head. "Marrying you isn't a heavy weight. It was never about you, Dylan. It was always about me. I'm scared about the thought of losing someone I love again."

He hugged her to him. "You won't lose me."

She lifted her head and looked up at him. "How can you say that, knowing what happened to Brian?"

"Nobody gets that kind of guarantee, Merry," he whispered softly. "You have to take a leap of faith and hope that life works out. In my experience, things do. You might end up going through a maze full of problems and loaded with worry, but you will come out the other end."

"You're so sure of everything."

He lowered his head until he was inches away from her face. She was scared, he could see it now, as clearly as he could see the amber in her irises. "I'm sure of you and me, and our family. Chloe and Spart, and the children I hope we will go on to have. That's all I need. Life doesn't come with guarantees, but I know this much—marrying you is the first step in the kind of life I never thought I could have. You make it possible, Merry. *You*." He pressed his lips against hers for a fleeting second, as if punctuating his sentence. "You and me, it begins with us. That's all I need."

She sighed out gently, and when her eyes glassed over, he thought she was going to cry. "That's all I need," she whispered. "You by my side."

"I'll always be right here." He hugged her again, firmly pressing his arms against her soft body, wanting to let her know that she was safe and protected, and she didn't need to be afraid.

Holding her like this, the grogginess of sleeping on the couch, the worry about getting to the workshop, disappeared. He had a chance to marry the woman of his dreams. There was no place for fear and worry in his world.

"She said we were meant to be together. That it was a blessing we had found one another."

He stared at her. "Who said?"

She breathed in sharply. "Ella Ray, the woman in the astrology shop a few doors down."

"You went there?"

She nodded and seemed to shrink back, as if he might judge her. He hadn't realized just how lost and confused she had been. She obviously had been, in order to go to a place like that. "But why?" he asked softly.

"I had a dream about Brian. I didn't tell you because I didn't want you to worry."

His heart tanked at the mention of her husband. He didn't mind that Merry needed more time, that she didn't want to rush things, but he was afraid that she might have doubts, and that scared him. The thought of losing her stabbed him like a knife.

"I woke up crying, and I thought it was real."

He hugged her, and listened as she told him how she had felt, and how she had taken everything going wrong as a sign of the universe hinting to her that she and Dylan shouldn't be together.

"That's what you thought?" he asked, finding it strange how they both differed in this one way. He didn't believe in these things, but Merry obviously had wanted answers and had been desperate enough to seek out Ella Ray's services. It made him even more scared. "What did she say?"

"She said you and I were supposed to be together. That we heal one another, and we're good for each other."

He breathed easier and suddenly had a newfound affinity for the astrology shop and its owner. Merry continued to tell him about her reading and how it had confused her and uplifted her.

"You needed a stranger to tell you that we're meant to be together?" he asked when she'd finished recounting her experience.

"Recent things have spooked me."

He'd noticed that. She panicked, and he would often be the one to calm her down, make her see that things weren't so bad, while she made him feel loved and warm, and filled his life with joy and all good things.

"I want to get married on the day we originally decided, Dylan."

"The *same* date?" he asked, lifting her chin up and forcing her to look at him. "Are you sure?"

She nodded.

"You realize that's *two* weeks away?"

"I know."

"You don't have a dress," he reminded her.

"I can get a dress. I have a huge list of sites to look through, once I get the girls on the case. I don't care about the dress."

He tried to tamp down his excitement, even though his heart felt as if it had suddenly been unshackled. "You were upset about the dress you wanted but couldn't get."

"I'm not sure it was about the dress."

He frowned, not understanding.

"I think it was about everything else, about this new journey you and I are about to go on together." She pressed her lips to his chest.

"You're ready for the ride now?"

"I'm ready, right now."

They smiled at each other, and for him, it was as if a huge, heavy boulder had been lifted from his chest. But he didn't want to give her expectations. Two weeks to turn everything around? Just before Christmas? They needed a miracle of epic proportions.

"I don't know if we can get the same date again. I'll have to check the venue and the caterers."

"I'll have to see if I can get a dress, and all the other things a bride needs."

"We have to tell everyone that it's back on," he said, knowing that they would have to get onto it super-fast.

"I have to tell my parents," said Merry.

"And I have to tell mine."

"Chloe will need a dress!"

"Good luck with that," he said, smiling.

She kissed him properly, igniting a fire in his belly, and reminding him that he needed to get on board with the honeymoon.

CHAPTER 23

"I'll wear anything, Mom, even pink, if you want me to."

Merry smiled, she hadn't really stopped smiling ever since Dylan had agreed. Odd, how making the right decision suddenly made the world seem brighter, lighter and simpler.

Her daughter had jumped for joy when they told her that they were getting married as originally planned. Luckily for them, the venue they had hired, then canceled, was still available, and the catering company was back in the game.

The preparations were moving forward at breakneck speed, and things went from ridiculously hectic to impossible. But these were good things, exciting things. None of it seemed like a heavy weight.

Once the decision had been made, Merry had felt weightless.

"I quite like the idea of a candy floss pink, tulle dress, and maybe ribbons in your hair. What do you think?" Merry asked.

Chloe was about to make a face, but grimaced a little. "What kind of ribbons?"

"I'm joking. Ribbons not required."

"Tulle?"

"Netting, like the skirt on a ballerina."

Her daughter's jaw dropped. Chloe disliked the very idea of such girly clothing. "For your wedding day, I'll do it," she said, as if Merry had asked her to drink a pint of bitter medicine.

"Again, I'm testing you, honey." Merry put her arm around her daughter's shoulder as they walked into the out-of-town department store. She was sure that they would find something, especially since Chloe seemed so accommodating.

It was her own wedding dress that she was worried about, and this weekend was her only chance.

Both sets of parents were arriving next week, and Dylan was still working in his workshop like a man possessed.

The rewards of a beautiful honeymoon awaited, he told her, although he wasn't giving her any hints about where they were going.

"Why are we going back to Whisper Falls?" she asked. With only two weekends to go before the wedding, getting a dress was the main priority today.

Jenna's eyes were on the road, her hands on the steering wheel. "You said you'd leave it to me," she said, glancing ahead.

Leigh giggled from the backseat. Merry turned, looked at Leigh then at Jenna whose eyes were still on the road. She was giving nothing away.

Her friends had been delighted when she had broken the news to them later in the evening on the day she and Dylan had decided to try for their original wedding date.

All the plans that her friends had put on hold were rolling forward again. Today, Jenna had insisted they would not come home until Merry had the perfect wedding dress.

In a way, she had been relieved that her friends were being so helpful. It took the burden and stress off her, which helped given the timeframe and all that was going on in the store.

Still, Merry had been surprised to see that they were heading back to the town, to the place where she'd had such a disastrous experience before.

Obviously, Jenna knew best, so she said nothing and instead looked at her lists to see what else she needed to get done.

"Is it the same shop?" Merry asked when they arrived at Whisper Falls again. Jenna couldn't stop grinning and looked as if she was about to explode from having to contain her excitement.

"Say nothing," Leigh advised her.

"Say nothing about what?" Merry asked.

"Just take a look," Jenna said as they stepped into the same shop.

"You go and wait outside the fitting room area," Jenna ordered. Merry lifted her eyebrow in protest, but Leigh took her by the arm and led her over to the comfy sofas next to the huge ornate mirror.

"What is Jenna up to?" she asked Leigh.

"You're about to find out."

In the next moment, Jenna appeared with a woman by her side. Someone Merry hadn't met before. The woman held out her hand, "Meredith Nicholls? Delighted to make your acquaintance. I'm Eloise, the owner."

Mild irritation bubbled up from Merry's stomach. This was the woman responsible for the whole wedding dress shambles? The woman apologized again and blabbered on, commiserating over the error her shop assistant had made.

"Your friend expressed your deep dissatisfaction and told us how upset you were."

Merry looked at Jenna, confused. Did this mean that dress, the one she had loved, was back on sale?

Eloise continued, "At least once a week, she would call us and ask if the wedding of the woman who had bought the dress you liked had fallen through."

"Jenna!" Merry had liked the dress, but not enough to wish someone's wedding had fallen through.

Jenna scowled. "I was only trying to help."

Merry braced herself, expecting to hear about the poor woman's misfortune and to be told that she could now have that dress again. Only, there was a slight problem now, she no longer wanted it. "You managed to get me that dress?"

"Thankfully, no," the shop owner replied. "That wedding is still on and that dress isn't available."

Merry felt relieved, but also perplexed.

"But we have another dress, similar in style, which your friend believes you might like even more."

Jenna clapped her hands together, looking and sounding like a six-year-old in the world's biggest toy shop.

Eloise clicked her fingers and from nowhere, a sales assistant stepped forward holding a wedding dress that was still on its hanger. Merry stood up, her mouth falling open as she glanced at the dress. It looked similar enough, only the beading was more intricate and the neckline not so plunging. She took in a few steadying breaths, not wanting to lift up her spirits, or get too excited.

With such a short time to go, she had resigned herself to getting a simple white full-length dress that 'would do.'

This, though, this vision of white satin and shimmering beads, this looked like something special.

She swallowed.

I won't get excited.

"Let me try it on," she said in the most level voice she could muster. But her body was already breaking out in goosebumps. The beads glistened under the lights. She took the dress from the sales assistant and felt the cool satin fabric against her fingers, noting its elegant style and shape.

This could be it.

She disappeared into the changing room, undressed, and slipped on the new dress. By the time the assistant had done up her zipper and Merry turned around to see herself in the mirror, her breath hitched in her throat.

She stepped back in shock at the first glance of her reflection in the mirror, and for a moment she forgot to breathe.

This. Was. It.

The dress.

The *perfect* dress.

Her wedding dress.

She felt on the verge of tears, and she couldn't understand why.

Running her hands over her figure, she turned around, admiring the way it hung on her, not too tight, but just right. And the bodice was perfect. She couldn't stop staring at herself, and at the same time, she was contemplating how things had come full circle. She had returned to this shop with no hope, but now she was wearing a dress that was simply perfect, and so much better than the one she had fallen in love with.

All thanks to her friends, and to Jenna especially.

She couldn't wait to see the look on Dylan's face when she walked down the aisle on her father's arm.

Shivers—of the good and excited kind—prickled her skin.

"What are you doing—" Jenna walked in with Leigh beside her and stopped mid-sentence. They both gasped out loud.

"Oh, honey." Jenna's face was a picture of delight.

"Merry," said Leigh. "*This* is your dress."

"I know," she said, her voice a whisper. "It's perfect. All of it. It fits." She peered at Jenna. "Did you get the alterations made?"

Jenna shook her head. "I swear, I didn't do a thing except hound Eloise every week."

"Even when the wedding was off?" Merry asked, surprised.

Leigh rolled her eyes. "Even when the wedding was off."

"You can talk," said Jenna, nudging her arm lightly. "As if you haven't had all the cake ingredients and the edible flowers ready to bake their wedding cake."

Leigh looked at Merry guiltily.

"You girls..." said Merry as a firework of happiness exploded in her stomach. "You girls are the best."

"You like it?" Jenna asked.

"What do you think?"

"I think she needs a bouquet to go with it," stated Leigh.

A bouquet. Merry groaned. Each time she crossed one thing off her list, more things were added to it.

"Luckily, my friend Mackenzie has been primed," said Leigh, gloating.

"Mackenzie?" Who was Mackenzie?

"The owner of Bloom, the florist in town. I can vouch for her flowers," said Jenna.

"Because Reed often buys her many," said Leigh.

"As if Rourke doesn't buy them for you," Jenna shot back.

"She can make you up something really nice," said Leigh. "You just have to come along with me and pick one."

Merry shrugged. Her wedding plans seemed to have taken on a life of their own. "I don't think I have a choice." She caught her reflection in the mirror and held her gaze.

She couldn't wait for Dylan to see her in this.

"If you ask me, I think it's a tragedy that you're not letting us throw you a bachelor party," said Rourke as he shoveled snow from Dylan's driveway.

"I have beer and I can put on music. I'm getting take-out later. What more do you want?" Dylan asked. Rourke straightened up and rested his hands on the shovel handle. His face was flushed and sweaty. "*This* isn't exactly the type of party I had in mind."

"I don't want to know what you had in mind," cried Reed from the ladder. He was still stringing fairy lights across the front of the house, and he'd just finished putting them up across the porch and terrace.

Dylan walked away to take a good look at his home, all decked out in golden lights. He hadn't turned them on yet, but he already knew that this would be a huge hit with his wife—for she would be his wife by the time she saw this.

Merry would love it.

He had never done this before, decked his house out in this way. Most years, he'd put up a small tree, but that was about it.

This year, everything had changed for him. There was something magical in getting married, especially at this time of year, and as soon as the snow had started to fall—a few days ago —he'd had the idea to decorate his entire home.

With her change in plans, Merry seemed content and at peace with December, and Christmas, and he wanted to double up on his efforts to ensure that all the bad memories of her past were completely overwritten with newer, happier ones.

"What do you think I had in mind?" Rourke shouted, clearly affronted. "Nothing but a few drinks, okay, a *lot* of drinks, and maybe a trip to the casino out of town."

"You think I've got money to throw away?" asked Dylan.

He'd worked around the clock, doing an insane couple of days recently, but he had managed to meet his vase order. He'd also managed to increase the inventory for the products sold at the store.

It had been truly insane and he was just glad that it was over.

Merry had forcibly removed him from the workshop yesterday, and with only two days to go before their big day, it was a good thing she had because he had started to unwind and relax, and he was finally was able to enjoy the wedding preparations.

"You don't have to bet the house," said Rourke and started shoveling snow again.

"Looking good," Dylan shouted out and gave a thumbs-up to Reed. "This is fun, isn't it?" Dylan asked Rourke as he walked back towards the house.

"Yeah, tons of fun," mumbled Rourke.

"This is enough. You don't need to shovel all of it. It looks pretty with snow everywhere."

Rourke wiped his forehead with the back of his hand. "The way it's going, everything's going to get covered up again overnight. There's more snow coming."

"Are you still going to be able to do the honeymoon trip?" Reed asked, climbing down from the ladder.

Dylan nodded. "There's no way we're not going on our honeymoon."

"It's a crying shame Merry won't fly," said Rourke.

"It's something she has to get over, something we can work on later." He had looked at hypnotherapy as a means for helping her getting over her fear of flying, but it was too soon to suggest anything like that now. After giving Chloe the Christmas morning she wanted, he and Merry would leave at noon and set off for their honeymoon. He had no plans to tell her until after they were married.

"She'll love it," Reed said, looking up at the house. "Do you need any more lights put up?"

"How many lights do you have?" Rourke asked. "'Cause I'm pretty sure you have at least a thousand up already."

"I don't want it to look overdone. This is just right. Shall we?" He reached for the controller switch in his pocket and turned the lights on.

Instantly, his home was transformed into a magical glistening wonderland. It looked even prettier with the snow all around.

"Wow!" Reed exclaimed.

"Holy shi—"

"Merry's going to love it," said Dylan, unable to stop himself from smiling. He couldn't wait to see the look on her face, and he couldn't wait to carry her over the threshold. "Let's call it a day, guys." He felt happy that everything on his list had been completed. "Let's go inside and crack open some beers."

Rourke threw down his shovel. "Now you're talking."

"Two days to go, buddy," said Reed as they walked into the house.

"I don't know where the time's gone." It had been a race against time, ever since Merry had once again expressed her wish to get married before Christmas.

Something had switched for her. Some ghosts had been laid to rest. He was glad he'd let her have the time to figure things out, glad he hadn't shown his disappointment when she'd first told him she wanted to postpone their wedding.

Things had worked out, just like he always knew they would.

"How many have you invited to the pre-wedding dinner?" Reed asked.

"About sixteen, I'm not sure who is definitely coming. Merry took care of the RSVPs. It's mainly just you guys, and Blake and Shay, and family."

Rourke almost choked on his beer. "Blake and Shay? Are they together?"

Reed nodded, before taking a sip from his beer. "Been dating a while, I think. Jenna says it was a surprise to her."

"I've seen them talking at the monthly meetings," said Dylan. "I'm not surprised."

"Speaking of monthly meetings, is Hyacinth coming to the dinner?"

Dylan shrugged. "I hope not. We didn't invite her, but she's friends with Merry's mom, so it won't surprise me if she ends up being there. Come early, guys, in case I need the support."

They'd booked a big table at Fellini's, and it would have been a huge gathering in itself, having such a large group of their friends and family at one event, but knowing that the wedding was the day after, and then their honeymoon would start the day after that put a smile on Dylan's face.

He was going to spend the rest of his life with Merry. Life certainly didn't get better than this.

"More food and drink," said Rourke patting his stomach, "I'll be there early. And all this before Christmas means that I'm going to have to watch my waistline."

"You're going to have to watch it anyway," said Dylan, "Merry and I don't know how you do it with all those cakes Leigh bakes."

"They're my downfall," Rourke agreed.

"Maybe I should thank my lucky stars that Jenna doesn't like to cook."

"But you have Cecile and her Southern fried chicken," Dylan reminded him.

"True."

He opened three bottles of beers, and they raised them high.

"To you guys. I don't know what I'd do without you," said Dylan.

"To you and Merry," said Reed.

"To an awesome honeymoon," said Rourke.

CHAPTER 24

*H*is nerves jangled wildly. He wasn't nervous. Just overexcited.

Today he was going to marry Merry.

The snow was still falling and had been on and off for the past few days. All of Rourke's hard work on decorating had been erased as a fresh carpet of snow formed all around his house again.

After an amazing pre-wedding dinner with family and friends filled with much laughter and cheer, they had gone home around midnight. Dylan had woken up early today and re-shoveled it first thing, hoping to at least clear some sort of pathway to his door so that he wouldn't fall flat on his face with Merry in his arms when he returned in the early hours of tomorrow morning.

After the wedding, there was a party in one of the banquet suites at The Grand Hotel, and it would go on until midnight. After a few days of more celebrations and spending Christmas morning with family, they would set off on the long drive to their honeymoon destination.

He wanted to fast-forward and get to their honeymoon cabin right now, but at the same time, he wanted to time to slow down, almost to a stop, so that he could savor each and every moment from this point on until the moment he exchanged vows with Merry and made her his wife. Vows which would bind them together, for better, for worse, for richer, for poorer, in sickness and in health.

He would love and cherish this woman until the end, but the end was far away, and not something he wanted to dwell on.

This was the start of their journey, and every tiny little thing, from the moment they had first clapped their angry gazes on each other, had led to this, their wedding day.

He dressed slowly, taking his time, not wanting to arrive at the church too early.

The beautiful old church looked even more pretty with its thick dusting of snow.

By the time he got there, his parents and Merry's, and other family and friends were all there.

His friends waited by his side, and he presumed that Merry would make her entrance with her father. Leigh and Jenna hovered inside the church doors, staying out of the falling snow. Every so often, they would look out to see if the Limo was coming.

"Nervous?" Rourke asked.

He shook his head. He wasn't nervous. Not in the slightest bit. Oddly, he felt the calmest he had in a while. It was as if the day was running in slow motion, and there was no rush to do anything but wait for his bride-to-be to arrive.

"*I'm* nervous," Rourke confessed.

"You're not even the one who's getting married," Reed said.

"But still. He's the first one out of us three to tie the knot. How in the heck is he not nervous?"

"I'm here guys, no need to talk about me as if I'm not here," said Dylan. A gasp from the women at the door made them all turn around.

"She's here!" Jenna cried.

"You'd better get to the front," Reed said, checking his watch. "Merry's right on time."

"Do you have the ring?" he asked his best man.

Rourke quickly shoved his hands in his pocket and nodded with a smile. Dylan hadn't been able to decide which of the two should be his best man. In the end, he'd had to toss a coin for it.

He walked to the altar, Rourke along with him, and waited for the wedding march to start.

Minutes passed, and still there was no music. After a few more moments had passed and the wedding march still hadn't started, panic set in.

Merry had arrived, but why was she taking so long? He turned to Rourke with a frown. "What's taking so long?"

"Relax, dude," his friend replied.

Rourke could relax, it wasn't his wedding. An uncharacteristic knot tied in Dylan's stomach. Could she be having second thoughts this late in the process? He felt his breath speed up, felt his insides hollow out.

Nerves.

Now he was starting to worry. Throwing a quick glance over his shoulder, he sought out Reed in the front. His friend jerked his head up at him, as if asking what was wrong.

Dylan shook his head, and Reed frowned back, as if not understanding. Dylan turned back to face the front. "Why is she taking so long?" he hissed to Rourke. He let out a sigh, tried to take a few deep breaths, tried to remind himself that things always worked out. But the mantra he had always lived by wasn't working this morning.

"Relax," Rourke answered back. "She'll be here. What's the worst that can happen, huh?"

Dylan scoffed at the line that Rourke tossed back at him. *His* line. He lowered his head as he faced the front and tried to breathe. If Merry had had second thoughts, if she'd bailed this close to the ceremony...

Just then the wedding march started, and his heart almost shocked right out of his ribcage.

It beat so loudly, he could feel the vibrations in his chest.

She was here, and she was coming. She was going to be his wife.

"Told you," Rourke whispered to him. Dylan glanced over his shoulder and got the first glimpse of his bride.

It blew him away.

Her amber eyes met his in a long, timeless moment. He didn't see anyone else, didn't hear anything. All he saw was Merry, looking incredibly beautiful.

And that dress.

The dress.

The dress.

The dress.

He tried hard not to give her an obvious up-and-down stare, but he had never, ever seen her look as lovely as she did right now. Her hair was up and swept away from her face, highlighting her features.

He couldn't breathe, couldn't think.

But his heart knew all that it needed to know. That she was his, and he was hers, and from this point on, they were one.

Mrs. Dylan Fraser walked out of the church, arm in arm with her new husband and feeling incredibly joyous as she smiled at the many happy faces all around them.

It had been the exact opposite of how she had felt when she'd stepped out of the Limo earlier. She had been so jittery and nervous as soon as she had arrived at the church that she had needed to take a moment to calm herself down.

Jenna and Leigh had helped her.

A sensation like butterflies going wild inside her ribcage made her restless and jumpy, made her feel as if it was too much.

But then she had taken a peek from the back, had seen Dylan standing facing the altar, and she had relaxed a little. She was going to marry this man who had brought her so much happiness. The man who had turned her world around, protected her, reassured her, rescued her.

She had taken in a long, calming breath.

"You've got this," Jenna whispered into her ear, while someone's hand, Leigh's, she presumed, rubbed her arm on the other side.

"Shall we, Meredith?" her father had asked, putting his arm out for her to take.

She did.

She walked in with her father, and found herself smiling, feeling calm, free from worry.

It was the look Dylan gave her, when he first turned and saw her, that filled her heart. Something in his expression gave away his sheer surprise, his admiration, his extreme joy.

She was aware only of him by her side as they took their vows, and before she could fully savor the moment, they were suddenly man and wife.

Blanketed by feelings of sheer joy, she left the church with her husband, indescribable happiness bubbling from her. The future she had always envisioned for herself—as one of growing older alone—faded into oblivion.

Spending the rest of her life with Dylan by her side was a beautiful way for her to embark on this next chapter of her life, one which she had never ever dreamed of when she had accepted her mother's offer to come to Starling Bay and help Hyacinth Fitzsimmons out.

She caught sight of the old, interfering busybody, and couldn't help but give her her best ever smile.

Once outside, they were soon surrounded by everyone congratulating them.

"Mommmm!" The sight of her daughter in a beautiful yellow lace was slightly marred by Chloe rushing towards them in an unladylike fashion. She hugged them both, and they barely managed to exchange a few words before their families and friends descended on them.

They had a moment, when it was just the two of them in the car being driven from the church to the hotel, to just be together and bask in their new way of being—a husband and wife.

"I got worried," Dylan said, clasping her hand firmly in his. "Why did you take so long to walk to the front?"

"Nerves."

He looked worried. "What do you mean 'nerves?' You weren't sure?" She clasped his hand in both of hers. "I was more than sure, but I had a rush of adrenaline. It was excitement."

"Are you sure?"

"You should know me by now. I panic, and then I get fretful, and then I'm okay. I'm always okay when you're with me."

He kissed the back of her hand. "You gave me a shock. I thought you'd bailed on me."

"Bailed?" she cried in exasperation. Even the driver looked in the rearview mirror. "You're the best thing to happen to me in years."

It was way past midnight by the time they had said goodbye to their parents. Her parents went home with Chloe, and Dylan's parents had gone back to their hotel room. Jenna and Leigh and their boyfriends and a handful of other friends still remained.

She had taken her shoes off and begged Dylan for one final dance, and when that was over, they said their goodbyes and left.

Dylan drove her home, back to his place. Snow had set thick and heavy everywhere, and as his pickup pulled up outside his house, she gasped.

"Your house looks so beautiful! *You* did that?" It was lit up with strands of lights all over the front and along the porch and terrace.

"Not me," he answered, smiling at her. "Reed and Rourke."

It looked truly magical, especially at this time of night, the fairy lights twinkling against the dark sky. She could do no more than look aghast at the house, unable to move. "Aw…It's beautiful. I love it. I really, *really* love it."

He'd gotten out of the truck and walked over to her side of the door, pulling it open.

"I knew you'd like it."

"I could sit here all night looking at it. It's so pretty."

"You can't sit here all night." Dylan reached in and slid his hand around her waist, surprising her. She leaned towards him and put her arms around his neck as he pulled her out of the truck with ease. "It's our wedding night."

Oh, yes. It certainly was. In answer, she flashed him her most inviting smile, and he dropped his head down and kissed her, standing out in the thick, crunchy snow with the quiet darkness all around them.

They had shared a moment slightly similar to this almost a year ago when they had been almost strangers, when he had rescued her.

"You can put me down now," she said, not expecting him to carry her through the snow.

"Heck, no. It's my prerogative." He started to walk with her through the snow, towards his door.

"To do what?"

"To carry you over the threshold."

He was insane, but he made her laugh. "It's snowing. We'll both fall over."

"I won't let you fall."

She stared at him, her insides turning warm and fluttery, even though she was outside in the cold. She knew he wouldn't ever let her fall. Knew he didn't mean it for just now in this moment, but forever. "Promise?"

"Promise. I won't ever let you go."

She giggled. "I love you, Mr. Fraser."

"I love you, Mrs. Fraser." He trudged through the ten-inch-thick snow, then fiddled with the key, and finally managed to open the front door before walking inside with her still in his arms.

She giggled loudly before burying her face in his neck and holding on for dear life.

And then she clung on, savoring the moment, inhaling his scent, relishing the feel of his hard body against hers.

They were married.

It would take some time getting used to this, and so she kept her face buried in his neck for a moment longer.

"Hey," he said when he tried to put her down but she still clung on. "I thought you wanted me to put you down."

She loosened her arms around him then and let him steady her onto the floor. He looked at her oddly.

"I was just trying to remind myself that we're married," she explained.

"New, isn't it?" he said, taking her hands and staring down at her.

She smiled back. "Where are we going on our honeymoon?"

"We're visiting someplace new. Somewhere you've never been, according to Chloe and your mom. A different country."

She blinked. "A different country?" She opened her mouth in dismay. "But Dylan, I can't fly."

He lowered his face, so that their noses were touching. "I know," he said, his sweet, hot breath caressing her cheeks. "We're driving to Canada. Montreal, in fact."

Her eyes widened. "We are?" She'd never been, but it sounded pretty and quaint. "Won't that take forever?"

"We'll leave at noon, and I'll drive carefully. We'll stop off at lots of different places along the way. It might take all day to get there, but we can talk and make our plans, and listen to the radio along the way."

She smiled, already loving the idea of it. In all their time together, they hadn't had much time alone to do these things, to just talk and just be, and make plans. She liked the sound of that. "But why don't we leave early?" she cried, "that way we can get there sooner."

His lips turned up at the corners. "Because it's our wedding night, and I don't plan on getting much sleep tonight."

She bit her lip, and smiled back, as his lips lowered to hers and he kissed her. Instinctively she put her arms around his neck again, and just like that, in the blink of an eye, he scooped her up in his arms and slowly climbed the stairs.

"It's *not* twins?" Chloe cried in disappointment when Merry and Dylan broke the news to her as soon as they returned from her hospital checkup.

"It's not twins," said Merry, releasing a huge sigh of relief. This time around, she had gained weight so fast that she had started to worry.

They had told Chloe and both sets of parents soon after she had gotten pregnant. And of course, their friends, Jenna and Reed, and Leigh and Rourke.

The increase in weight had alarmed her, and many a time she'd wondered and feared that she might be having twins.

"Aw, that would have been so much fun," said Chloe, sounding as if she'd obviously grown used to the idea. Merry looked at Dylan in surprise.

"Maybe for you, sweetie," she said to her daughter. "But two babies at once would be too much for me to handle."

"I could have babysat them both. I still will babysit. So?" Chloe asked. "What is it?"

"We don't know. We didn't *want* to know." She and Dylan had decided beforehand that they wanted a surprise.

"Why do you want twins?" Dylan asked.

"So that I could have a brother *and* a sister all at once."

"Honey," said Merry, hugging her daughter. "It doesn't work like that."

"I know, Mom. But you never know." Chloe turned away to look at her cell phone which started ringing just then. "Dawn's coming tonight for a sleepover, I forgot to tell you. Is it okay?"

"I guess it is now."

"Thanks, Mom." Chloe answered the call as she rushed away.

"Happy now?" said Dylan, smoothing his hand over her belly. He did that a lot, kissed her belly at night before he went to bed. She found it amusing, his wonderment at her pregnancy. The baby wasn't kicking yet, but she could just imagine his delight when that started.

"Yes. I feel better now." Now that she'd had her checkup and everything was fine, and it was only one baby.

"Shall we sit outside?" Dylan suggested, then took her hand when she nodded and walked outside to the porch.

They sat here most evenings now that it was summertime. After dinner it was better and slightly cooler, too. She loved the view, acres of land spreading out like a lush green carpet before them. They had moved into their new home two months after their wedding. This house had come on the market soon after they had returned from their honeymoon, and she and Dylan had taken one look at it and fallen in love with it at first glance.

Most things in her life had fallen into place, what with the wedding and the new house, and finally, a new baby that was due in December. She had never intended for it to be that way; they had been trying for a child ever since their wedding night, but a Christmas baby was what it was going to be.

Sometimes, no matter what, life had its own plans.

By the time the baby came, it would be their first wedding anniversary. It would also be two years from the time she had first come to Starling Bay, needing to escape the hectic pace of life in Boston.

What a wonderful trip that had been. A trip she had almost never made, had never really *wanted* to make, and yet it had turned everything around for her. She had met Dylan and started over. And now she couldn't envision a life without him by her side.

She relished the thought that he would be with her forever, through good times and bad, at every step of the way. That he would be her friend, her lover, her rock. And she would be the same for him.

Life had certainly never looked better, and now, instead of worrying about the future, she welcomed it. There was much to be grateful for. Much to look forward to. A lifetime of new memories to make and cherish.

Thank you for reading *Winter's Vow*!

I hope you enjoyed the follow-up to Dylan and Merry's story after they first met in Winter's Kiss.

Guarded Hearts is the next book in this series. It's another standalone romance and features Roxy from the diner. Expect to hear from some of the other characters in this story as well. You can read an excerpt at the end of this book.

If you'd like to be notified of new book releases and more, please subscribe to my newsletter here:

http://www.siennacarr.com/newsletter

Thank you,

Sienna

EXCERPT FROM GUARDED HEARTS

CHAPTER 1

ailey Ross opened her gold cosmetic mirror and checked to see if her lipstick needed touching up. She turned her head to the left and right, frowned at the sight of newly formed fine lines on the corners of her eyes, and checked to see if the red matte color on her as yet naturally full lips was fine.

She was starving; the few slices of cucumber and lettuce she had had for brunch had done nothing to appease her hunger and her stomach gurgled while Val, her publicist and agent, feasted on eggs Benedict and salmon slathered over with a creamy looking butter-colored Hollandaise sauce.

Inside, she was salivating, as well as slowly dying a little each time Val lifted her fork to her mouth. Hailey looked away, choosing to focus on the potted palm trees dotted around the shimmering blue pool at the Beverly Wilshire Hotel.

"Bruce will go with you," Val announced.

"I don't need a bodyguard. I'm going back to my hometown. Nothing ever happens there." It simply wasn't necessary. She only ever needed bodyguards for large crowds and at events like movie premieres where prestigious jewelers loaned her glitzy and ridiculously expensive pieces of jewelry.

"You're taking Bruce and that's that. No buts." She was about to protest further but she knew that when Val put her foot down, there was usually a good reason for it. Hailey's insides slumped. The timing was lousy. She had her eyes on a few meaty movie roles she had auditioned for. There was also the fact that she didn't relish the idea of returning to Starling Bay, a place she had long ago put behind her.

The release of her latest movie, the third in her successful Monica Martins franchise, had been delayed by six months due to a horrific helicopter crash involving the director and several members of the cast. Luckily, she hadn't been aboard the flight. The director's life had hung in the balance but he was now on the long road to recovery. The movie had finally released and the premiere had taken place in LA last month.

Unfortunately, she now had to attend a second movie premiere in Starling Bay.

To compound matters, one of the TV networks had signed to produce a documentary covering her life story from her years as a gawky teen with humble beginnings in the small town she had grown up into where she was now, a Hollywood A-lister. This also had been delayed. She had been secretly hoping that the TV network would hold off on the documentary, but they seemed as eager as ever for it to go ahead. There was no way out of it. She had to return to her hometown.

She hated the thought of her bodyguard tagging along with her. Bruce would stick out like a sore thumb with his sinister-looking dark suit and shades. She tried once more to appeal to Val. "It's really not necessary for Bruce to tag along."

"You can drop him once you've finished filming the documentary and the premiere is over."

"But it's only in Starling Bay!"

"It's a condition of the studio, Hailey. Please don't keep going on about it."

"What is it?" Hailey asked. Val was holding something back. "Is it the letters? Did they start up again?" In the last few months, she had been receiving letters from one particular fan. These weren't like the types of letters she was used to—friendly and full of admiration. This fan professed his undying love for her and got angry about the villains in her movies. Val had obviously been concerned about it enough to beef up the security at the main events.

"No. They haven't started up again."

"You'd tell me, wouldn't you?"

"Of course I would tell you."

It was normal in her line of work to attract a fair share of weirdos; it was part of the package for being in the public eye, for taking on the sort of acting roles she did where she was eye candy. Curves and long legs. The Monica Martins action movie franchise in which she played a feisty heroine on various quests in remote parts of the world had propelled her to another level of fame. Too bad her outfits consisted of the shortest of shorts and skimpy tops. No man in a similar role, save for Tarzan, would be expected to wear such skimpy clothing in such harsh places and climates. It seemed to be only the women who were expected to wear such things—another reason for her wanting to move away from these cheesy roles and look for something more serious.

Her security detail had been beefed up in recent months and while Val had refused to show her the letters—not that she had particularly wanted to see them—the extra protection wasn't something she welcomed.

"Then there's nothing to worry about."

Val set down her silverware and shifted her shades further along her head. "There's absolutely nothing to worry about, but the studio is going to give me grief if I let you go alone. Just take Bruce, pretend he's invisible and enjoy your visit."

Hailey snorted. Returning to Starling Bay after so many years didn't feel like an enjoyable visit. "I'll be bored sick in no time." Her life back then, as a tall and skinny teen, had been boring in comparison to her life now. She had towered above others at school and had found herself the center of unwanted attention from boys. At the age of thirteen, a TV scout discovered her during his visit to Starling Bay. A photoshoot followed, and then she got a bit part in a TV commercial. Not long after that she was lucky enough to try out for a children's TV show. With her sparkling blue eyes, blonde hair and charming smile, it was enough to get her the role. When the bright lights and glamor of Hollywood had beckoned, she left.

But returning to that same small town was a different matter. Now she was afraid of not fitting in, of causing a commotion, of old memories from a less pleasant time resurfacing.

On the flip side, she was still recovering from the exhausting post-release and publicity schedule, appearing in TV shows in order to promote the movie. In that respect, maybe spending some time in a small town wouldn't be such a bad thing.

"Oh, and you have a signing event at the local mall. I'll deal with the management there and have the appropriate merchandise sent over."

"What merchandise?" Two events to deal with were bad enough, and now Val was adding a third.

"Monica Martins swag, I'll put something together with the marketing department. You just have to look pretty and sign autographs and be nice to your fans."

"I'm always nice to my fans."

Val tapped her finger thoughtfully on the long stem of her glass. "I'm just wondering …"

Hailey braced herself. Val could come up with some hairbrained ideas sometimes. "Wondering about what?"

"Whether we should have Big Rock show up to surprise you."

She clenched her jaw tightly. This was the second time in as many weeks that Val had brought up Big Rock, her friend and a former child star whom she had known from her first TV show. He was quickly climbing the ranks of Hollywood royalty thanks to his huge summer blockbuster hit. The name had stuck because he was a huge guy of Herculean proportion, and he'd been called Rock in the teen show. His real name was Rick Moretti. She was happy for him and his success, especially because it had been long overdue, but she was also aware that the studio liked to put people together in the hopes of driving fans wild with false rumors. "Why?"

"It's good publicity. You guys have been seen out and about."

"We've been catching up. We know one another. We have friends in common."

"You certainly photograph well together," Val remarked.

She balked at the idea. Val had been after her to do more publicity stunts with Rick ever since a photo taken at an awards show—when she had presented him with an award—had gone viral. Because they knew one another, their chemistry that night—both when she kissed him on the cheek to give him the award, and at the after-party later—seemed to have caught a mood. They looked good together; there was no doubt about that. Big Rock was tall, like her, but dark-haired and muscular. He was handsome in a rugged way, with dark brown eyes and an attitude. The media had gone wild. While she could see how they were a celebrity magazine's dream couple, there was no chemistry, not that anyone would have noticed. Surface level was all that counted in Hollywood.

It was never anything deeper, but ever since that night, Val had started suggesting that she and Big Rock do some publicity stunts together, or accidentally show up at the same bar and restaurant where, magically, paparazzi would be waiting.

She had been horrified by the suggestion, and though Val hadn't said it in such direct terms, Hailey was all too aware that a fake romance could help with the buzz of publicity.

Hailey didn't like the idea of that and she did not want any part of this. "No. Please don't bring that up again."

"Okay, fine. But *I* would love to spend a week in Starling Bay," exclaimed Val, sliding her sunglasses onto her face again. "It's *such* a pretty little place." Val had visited Starling Bay when she had a week's vacation time to use up. She had gone with her boyfriend and come back in love with the town.

Hailey folded her arms and stared at the sunshine reflecting off the calm surface of the swimming pool. She couldn't deny that. It was a pretty place, but LA was home. Palm trees and sunshine. Poodles and high heels. Cocktails under glittering night skies. Sometimes, when the pace got to be too much here, she took off to her second home in Santa Monica. Not bad achievements for a twenty-four-year-old. She was super successful and hugely popular, for *now*—while her latest movie was riding high on its new release ratings, but unless her *next* one did well—and the one after that, and the one after that—she would be forgotten in time. She would still be rich, though not as famous, and over time she would definitely be forgotten.

"I've booked you a suite at The Grand Hotel. It's busy and central, but it has the standard of luxury you're used to."

"I don't want busy." She wanted to avoid fans and forget the disadvantages of fame.

"I could rent you one of those delightful houses by the bay, or you could stay in one of the condos at Forest Heights, a luxury development. I think it's too far. Central is best. I'll feel better knowing that you're in the heart of the town center."

"Why don't you come out with me?" Hailey asked.

"Because I'm working on your behalf here."

Hailey sat upright in her chair. "Be sure to let me know the moment you hear back about the schoolteacher audition."

Val sipped from her glass of sparkling water and made a face. Hailey knew it wasn't from the sharp taste of too much fizz. "Monica Martins makes you rich. Getting that schoolteacher's role will confuse your fans."

"Julia Roberts managed it." She had her heart set on the role. It would be so different than the roles she currently had.

"But *Pretty Woman* made her, and Pretty Woman she'll be for life."

"She doesn't care," Hailey protested. "She's made her fortune, and now she can play whatever parts she wants."

"Julia who?" Val cupped a hand to her ear.

Life in Tinseltown could be fickle. Maybe a visit to someplace more laidback was the thing she needed.

Guarded Hearts is available at all major retailers.

BOOKLIST

Whirlwind Kisses
Winter's Kiss
Maid for Him
Love Letters
Escape to Starling Bay (Books 1-3)
From Faking to Forever
Winter's Vow
Guarded Hearts
Table for Two
A Bouquet of Charm
Christmas Hope

For a complete list of books go to:
http://www.siennacarr.com/books

ACKNOWLEDGMENTS

I would like to thank my amazing group of proofreaders who check my manuscript for errors, typos and inconsistencies.

I am eternally grateful for their help and support. A special thanks to Dena and Nancy for their creative input with this story!

Dena Pugh

Charlotte Rebelein

Carole Tunstall

I would also like to thank Tatiana Vila of Vila Design for creating the awesome cover.

ABOUT THE AUTHOR

Sienna Carr is the sweet romance pen name for an author who has been writing romance since 2013. She lives in the UK with her husband, three children, and a parrot.

Connect with Me

I love hearing from you – so please don't be shy!

You can email me at: sienna@siennacarr.com

www.ingramcontent.com/pod-product-compliance
Lightning Source LLC
Chambersburg PA
CBHW020816190726
48285CB00006B/2308